Be Careful What You Wish For

Other Books by Jennifer Friess

The Wind Could Blow a Bug

When You Least Expect It

Be Careful What You Wish For

The Riley Sisters

Book 3

By Jennifer Friess

Mr. Ugly-Man Entertainment
Adrian, Michigan

Mr. Ugly-Man Entertainment
Adrian, Michigan
First Edition January 2016
Text copyright ©2016 by Jennifer Friess
All Rights Reserved, including the right of reproduction in whole or in part in any form.
To book an event or to purchase additional copies, please visit:
imnotstalkingyou.com

ISBN 9780692549124

To Masen, my son, the other part of my heart that I didn't even know was missing.

EVERYONE IS WATCHING AND THEY JUST DON'T

Any time you cry
It is captured on two TV screens
The mucous clot in your throat grows bigger
suffocating you
It all hurts worse now
You used to think
No one saw
No one noticed
THAT
Was why no one came to rescue you from the castle of
impossible dreams
But now you know the truth
Everyone is watching
Everyone sees
And they just don't care
You'll have to rescue yourself
But that is just another impossible dream
--JLF 10/2/01

MILEY

"Just take a deep breath. We have it all under control."

"HOW CAN YOU SAY THAT?! This is MY WEDDING, NOT YOURS! There is no cake, no groom, and it is going to rain on my outdoor reception," the young bride collapsed in tears into Miley's arms.

"Vanessa, you have to stop this. You will ruin your makeup. We have sent a car to go fetch the groom. He wants to be here, but his car broke down. It is the ones that don't want to be married that are the hardest to resolve. And twenty years from now, all you will see in the pictures are your makeup and the groom. So, you see, your job is to stop crying. Let us take care of the rest," Miley reassured her.

"But the rain—," the bride insisted.

"I once attended a wedding that got hit by a tornado, and it all turned out OK. We have tents being erected as we speak."

"Tents? In the yard?" The bride dashed to the bedroom window to confirm the news. Now she began to cry again; this time with tears of joy.

Little did the bride know that Miley had actually ordered the tents a week ago, based on the extended weekly forecast. The outdoor reception would certainly need them. The uncertain part was that until the bride's father actually saw the impending storm clouds blossoming in the sky for himself, he wouldn't agree to pay the added cost.

"What did I say was your only job today?" Miley reminded her.

"To not cry," Vanessa the bride squeaked, smiling now at Miley. The bride stared up at Miley, her big brown eyes reflecting her helplessness like a cow at the county fair. After a year of planning, Vanessa was finally going to put her trust in Miley to successfully complete the task she was hired to do.

"That's right. I am going to send your bridesmaids in here to keep you cal—company. I have to go tie-up a few last-minute details."

"Were you really at a wedding that survived a tornado?"

"Yes. A few buildings in town were destroyed, but no one died. A lovely time was had by all," she replied flippantly. Miley didn't mention that she had only been fifteen years old and a guest at said event.

With that, Miley quickly excused herself from the room. She selected a number from the contact list on her cell phone. A voice quickly responded from the other end of the call through the earpiece in her ear.

"Is the five-tier vanilla with vanilla buttercream on its way?" An affirmative response came from the other end.

"Did you have time to add some red flowers?" Another yes.

"Thanks. You are a lifesaver. You always come through for me with backup cakes." Miley had an in with a baker who kept a stash of frozen cakes and an employee on-call at all times. Cake disasters were not common, but were always enough to send an already anxious bride over the edge. Usually a few accents in the wedding colors could be added to an all-white cake. And no one pays attention to the flavor when it is being smashed in their face. She pushed a button and silenced the phone as she hit the bottom of the stairs.

After finding the bridesmaids at the back door smoking pot, she sent them up to be with Vanessa. While Miley did not blatantly suggest it, she hoped they would share their stash with the keyed up bride.

Miley made sure the wedding guests had begun to file into the downstairs of the house. She had personally never been in a house where the dining and living spaces could be opened up large enough to hold so many people. Even more would be arriving for the reception. That was saying something, as she had been in many lavish homes in her career of party planning.

"Just as long as the groom arrives," Miley thought to herself. She pushed through a side door and cut across the impeccable lawn, taking a shortcut over to the reception tents. But she wasn't quick enough.

"Miss Riley!" someone shouted from behind her. She held up her tablet to block her face and shield her from the shouter. She assumed it was probably the father of the bride. She knew her action was rude, but if he really wanted everything to go off without a hitch, he would let her check on the essentials. Miley had learned a long time ago from her mentor and business partner Jenny Jones, "Take care of the essentials, and the details will fall into place." All the hardest challenges always happened before the ceremony began.

Miley's light pink dress that came just above the knee flowed behind her as she hurried down the sidewalk, her high heels clicking all the way. She was glad she had chosen a sleeveless dress and worn her hair up. The humidity had been near one hundred percent all morning. She knew the impending storm would cool off the southern evening some, but never enough.

"I bet you are ready for vacation," Travis yelled across the tables to Miley. She made a beeline over to him.

Travis Masen was a caterer that Miley used regularly when she was doing jobs close to home, such as in Huntington or Oakley. He was a great caterer. He made great food. He was very reliable. And he was Miley's best friend.

Miley knew that after the cost of food, the delivery truck, advertising, and paying his employees, Travis didn't make a ton of money from catering. But he was a bachelor who knew how to pinch a penny. And he drove a motorcycle, so that didn't take much gas. Anything for the business was a potential tax write-off. He did make enough that he didn't have to work any other jobs for anyone else.

He hoped to one day get a store front. Not only would he be able to have access to industrial kitchen equipment that he did not have now, but he could also serve some of his specialties in a café-type atmosphere to customers off the street.

Travis used to be a skateboarder. It was still evident in his long shaggy blond hair and the baggy clothes he wore on his days off. Miley always thought of him as a "skate rat," but she couldn't remember if that was a derogatory term or not, so she only used it in her head. He probably would still be hanging with that crowd, not doing much of anything with his life, if he had not found his love of cooking.

Travis was mostly self-taught. Miley asked him once if that meant he just sat around and watched a lot of the Food Channel. He scoffed at Miley. He tried to explain how cooking had to be experienced by the five senses. He claimed you couldn't know how to prepare food until you felt the textures with your hands. He told her you couldn't smell onions sautéing through a television screen. He was right; at least until next year, when the Smell-O-Vision 5000 hits stores. She didn't really understand what he was getting at. But she did always enjoy eating the results.

Occasionally, he could still be seen riding his skateboard through the park on a cool evening at twilight. Miley didn't understand the hobby. When she was driving and saw an assemblage of youth hanging out skateboarding, she turned up her nose at them. Just a waste of time. No value to it.

But when she saw Travis on his board, she never thought those things. It was the one time he truly looked free; even more so than when he was cooking. Miley suspected that is how he probably started skateboarding—to have freedom from his mother's watchful eyes, to control when he came and went. Miley saw that board as the gateway drug to his motorcycle. He wanted to be sure he could go anywhere he wanted to—alone, without his mother following. Miley had ridden on his motorcycle with him a few times. But she missed her radio. And air conditioning.

"This job might kill me before I make it to the airport," Miley told him, a little too loudly. She looked around to make sure no one from the wedding party had heard. It was very poor customer service to bitch about your client while still at their residence. But this had been a brutal plan from day one. The event fell on a day when Jenny was unable to assist. It also fell the day before Miley's vacation, which was enough to almost break her. Almost.

"So, you are really leaving me for sunny Los Angeles?" Travis cocked his head to the side in that way he always did, his sandy blond hair shifting to hang in his eyes. He rolled another aluminum food warmer, what he always referred to as a "hot box," over near the table it would be unloaded onto. Travis moved heavy containers of food and often helped move furniture for events, but he never seemed to develop any more muscle tone. He was skinny, but not tall enough to be lanky. He was a year older than Miley.

"Hells, yes," Miley said emphatically.

"You know I hate it when you use that expression." Travis gave her a sour look.

"Two whole weeks. I can't remember the last time I took a real vacation. It is going to be so fun hanging out with my sister Kiley."

"Don't spend all your time stalking the stars. We don't want another incident like last time," he stated.

"What? There was no incident when we waited in the parking lot of the sports arena until GC came out. There was the bodyguard nazi, but we outwaited her lies that the band would never come out."

"No, I'm talking about when you went to Rod Hadley's home and sat in his driveway for three hours until you saw him come out of the house with his gun," Travis reminded her.

"Oh, ya, well. There was that. But he never filed any formal charges... that I know of," she shook her head, recalling the experience again. "That totally scared me off of rock gods for good."

"You just remember to come back home again, capeesh?" Travis stated pointedly. Travis knew better than anyone how a trip to Hollywood for Miley was like a trip to the liquor store for an alcoholic.

Miley dreamed bigger. She felt she was destined for more than merely some office job like her mother had toiled away at. Her dreams had always resided in the entertainment industry, although she had no specific talents of her own to exploit. But that is what was so great about living in the age of reality TV. Anyone could be discovered at any time. Maybe right now an executive wanted a reality show about an Alabama party planner!

"Oh, you'll just have to wait and see." Miley smiled at him, then headed back into the house to start the ceremony as the first raindrops started to fall. She could see the groom through the French doors that overlooked the garden. He was fussing with his hair and then his vest, flustered from having arrived so late.

This would be another success to add to her physical portfolio and her mental ego boost.

As the event was winding down, Miley headed out to find Travis to tell him to pick up her mail while she was gone. If he had already left, she supposed she could text him. Or mention it on their bedtime call, which had become routine between the two of them.

Miley soon lost her train of thought when she saw an attractive man sans shirt loading the catering truck. Miley thought she knew all the employees who worked for Travis, but this guy must be new. It was still warm and muggy after the rain. As she approached, she could see the moisture from the air clinging to the well-defined muscles in his back that moved as he worked. He turned so that she was able to see his nice chest and abdomen, but a box still blocked his face. Holding the box made his biceps bulge under the strain. She felt her whole body flush with the warmth of attraction. He was so yummy Miley wanted to lick him. Or bite him. Or both.

"Ooo, who is that hunk?" Miley asked a server named Tanya.

"Who?" she asked, perplexed. "I only see Travis over there. You know Travis."

As the man in question turned and put down the box, Miley could plainly see who it had been. Duh, of course Miley knew Travis.

"Oh, he must have walked away. Thanks, though," Miley quickly covered.

Making goo-goo eyes at Travis? What was she thinking? She really needed to get laid again soon before her indiscriminate lusting really got out of control.

2

It was all Miley could do to crawl out of bed and drag herself and her over-stuffed luggage downstairs to meet Kiley to leave for the airport. Neither Miley nor Kiley had ever been early risers. Growing up, their mother had sometimes resorted to using a plant mister to get them out of bed on Saturdays for long-distance cheerleading competitions. She wondered how Kiley had managed to get up so early. Kiley had already been on the road for two hours, driving up to Huntington from the farm she lived on with her boyfriend in Oakley. She must have been even more excited than Miley.

After all, it was Kiley's book being turned into a movie. Or, to make it sound more important, her debut novel was being shot for a feature film. That is how Miley phrased it to all her friends.

Miley was quite jealous of this. Miley thought she was doing good owning (OK—co-owning) a highly successful party planning business. But somehow her baby sister had shown her up. Miley hungered to be famous. How other people desired wealth enough to drive themselves to the poor house buying lottery tickets was akin to the level of her entertainment obsession. She simply hadn't had many chances in rural Alabama to fulfill her aspirations.

Kiley's name now showed up once in a while in the very Hollywood entertainment magazines that Miley had fantasized of being in herself someday when she was a child. Of course, usually it was a tiny blurb under the pictures of the fresh-faced unknowns starring in the movie, with a caption such as "Bobby Patterson and Christy Stevens star in the film adaption of K. Riley's best-selling book *Don't Judge a Boy by His Shoes*."

Yes, there was no way Miley was going to miss out on this trip. She couldn't wait to get to Tinseltown. To visit the mythical, magical Hollywoodland...

"Wake up, dork. We are at the airport. And you owe me seventy dollars for long-term parking," Kiley grumbled.

"You are the one with the major motion picture. Why should I have to chip in?" Miley stifled a yawn. The car was now parked on some level of a massive parking garage.

"You are the successful business owner. And you know I invested most of the money I made from the sale of the rights to JT and Associates Development."

"That is only a fancy way to say you gave several grand to your fiancé."

"Josh is not my fiancé!" Kiley argued.

"Oh, it is only a matter of time."

"Possibly. But that time hasn't arrived yet. And I am fine with that." They both got out of the car and gathered their luggage. The headlights flashed and the car's horn echoed against the concrete walls, signaling Kiley had locked it, as they began to head for the terminal.

"Do you know how much it sucks to be twenty-five years old and have no husband and no marriage prospects? No, of course you don't. Let me tell you, it sucks big balls." Their suitcases rolled behind them, a steady drone of plastic wheels being worn down by the abrasive floor.

"What happened to Sandy?" Kiley asked.

"My on-again, off-again boyfriend? He is off-again. Most likely forever. He actually moved out this time."

"I'm sorry."

"Don't be. We are heading to California! Where I am going to find me a new man. A rich man. Maybe a star...," Miley pondered, slipping on her sunglasses, despite the fact that it was still pre-dawn, and taking the lead ahead of Kiley.

"Mile, could you be any more shallow?" Kiley asked her sister.

"Mmm," Miley pretended to think about it. "Probably not."

Miley was very disappointed by the appearance of the other passengers on the airplane. She had made sure to nurture the perfect tan as preparation for her vacation. Her home manicure still looked fresh, having applied it shortly before the wedding. She also had freshened up the highlights in her long dark blond hair. It now came halfway down her back. It was wavy now, because she had left the house while it was still wet. But she had made sure she brought her flat iron as well. Was straight still the go-to look in Hollywood? Man, she hated trying to cultivate glamorous style on a tight budget.

All the other passengers simply looked like the everyday Joes she would pass at the pharmacy or the mall. She couldn't say grocery store, because she never went there unless it was a special occasion, like if she was planning a picnic or something. Miley didn't understand how people could take their whole family, towing grandparents and a gaggle of children, and spend hours at such an establishment. She was the kind that did all her weekly shopping in fifteen minutes at the chain pharmacy on the corner. She could walk the whole store in less than one minute. They had makeup, toilet paper, the bare necessities of food, such as granola bars. What else did a person need?

Other people painted pictures or assembled model battleships as hobbies. Miley's hobby had always been following Hollywood. No matter what she was going through or how bad her day had been, the celebrities within her movie magazines were always smiling back at her. Her favorite movie never deviated from the same course of action, no matter how unlikely the actors in the romantic pairing or their circumstance.

Miley sometimes day-dreamed that a good-looking, famous actor would find himself in Huntington and have a need for some party-planning. Or sometimes, she would fanaticize about simply running into a celebrity on the street or in the coffee shop. Then they would have a brief courtship, where he would buy her lots of expensive gifts. Then, well, he would sweep her off her feet and out to Los Angeles to live with him happily ever after. It would be like a romantic comedy, except it would leave out the usual misunderstanding that drives the two lovers apart before they are reunited again in the final act. Miley fell asleep every night with these scenarios running through her head. She could recast a new hunk when it was convenient. She wondered if that is how everyone put themselves to sleep at night.

In her mind's eye, she had envisioned a plane full of movie stars and models. But she guessed that was unrealistic, since she was on a Huntington to Los Angeles flight. If it had been a NYC to LA flight, maybe that would have been different. Maybe a flight like that would carry a guy who would try to flirt with her. Then she could blow him off. Then he would reveal that he was a talent agent and he had just "discovered" her. People got discovered in odd places all the time. Pamela Anderson had been discovered when she appeared on the JumboTron at a football game, wearing the right shirt. Not that Miley wanted to follow Pam's same path to fame, but she wasn't against using anything she had to her advantage. Miley sighed.

"What are you grinning about, you goofball?"

Kiley's comment snapped Miley out of her daydream.

"Nothing. I was just thinking of all the different ways I have envisioned this trip in my head."

"And let me guess. It probably involves a guy."

Miley shrugged. "I plead the fifth."

Miley knew that her identical twin sister Kiley thought of her as selfish. Kiley had made no secret of that since they had turned fourteen and their personalities had diverged. Kiley always told it that they both changed. Miley believed only Kiley had. Kiley had begun to make fun of the things that they had always both loved. Miley still felt an undeniable connection with her twin. But she had never forgiven Kiley for this, what Miley viewed as a betrayal.

Not only did Kiley's tastes change at that time, but her appearance as well. Kiley cut her hair and dyed it black. She began listening to alternative music and dressing goth. At college, her clothing had gone from goth to grunge, but whatever. Miley guessed people at college must have all the style sucked out of them. She wouldn't know. She had skipped college and worked on building a business instead.

Up until recently, Kiley had still worn her hair dyed jet black, cut into a bob with severely straight bangs. In the last year or so, she had finally grown out the bangs and let it go back to its natural light brown. It now came down to almost her shoulders, so that she could actually get it into a ponytail on occasion.

Jenny Jones, who already was running the business quite well on her own, was kind enough to take Miley on as an apprentice when she had expressed an interest. Jenny worked full-time as the librarian in Oakley, the tiny town where Miley had grown up. Jenny also had a new husband and they were trying to start a family, even though she was getting on in years. All this helped to convince Jenny that she should then take Miley on as a full partner. Miley showed such a knack for marketing and networking that soon she was probably doing more work than Jenny was. But Miley wasn't bitter about that. Much. Miley did realize it would have taken her years to start her own company and build it up to where Jenny had hers when Miley was hired. Jenny had done all the hard start-up work and reputation-building. All Miley had to do was tweak the existing processes, spread the word about their great services to anyone who would listen, and make sure their ideas didn't get stale.

3

The flight landed at LAX around 11:00AM. It took another hour before they were out of the airport. Miley was famished. Her stomach was still on Alabama time. She wanted to grab a bite in the airport, but Kiley insisted that they wait. The movie company, Plateau Studios, was sending a car for them, and then they were all to have lunch at some fancy restaurant. Miley had seen the small portions such places could serve while watching TV shows such as *Sex and the City*. She was so hungry, she figured she could probably down two hot dogs in the airport and still eat a polite amount at their destination as well. But soon they had their luggage and found the man at the designated entrance in front of a black luxury sedan holding a sign which read "Riley."

They were chauffeured on the freeways drawing them in closer like a spider's web to Los Angeles. Miley felt like her skin had been scraped with sandpaper; all her nerve endings were hyper-aware. The light, the air, the people—they all seemed different out here. Miley didn't know how Kiley felt right at this minute, but Miley believed she could go into stimuli overload any second.

The driver explained that he would take a longer route, allowing them to pass some of the better known landmarks. They were on the 101. Miley caught a glimpse of the famous white Hollywood sign. She dug through her carry-on for her cell phone. Miley had quickly tossed it into the bowels of the bag at the airport. There was so much stuff in her bag for the trip that was not normally in her day-to-day purse that she couldn't find it. The tears of excitement in her eyes clouded her vision. By the time she found it, the iconic sign had hidden itself behind towering buildings and palm trees. It continued to play peekaboo with her in this way. Kiley assured her they would be back later to sightsee. Tears continued to silently slip from Miley's eyes. Luckily Kiley said nothing.

Miley saw street signs and stores she had seen a million times in movies. The corner of Hollywood and Vine. Grauman's Chinese Theater. She couldn't take her eyes off the buildings as they drove west into the studio zone. Historically, it was the easiest place to film everything for most of the twentieth century, financially speaking. They traveled past CBS Television City. And they passed numerous stores with names she was used to, but occupying oversized opulent buildings that didn't seem to match.

Their lunch was to be at one of those Hollywood hot spots Miley saw nightly on OMGz, the daily celebrity gossip television show. The place where stars went to be seen, but pretended that they didn't want to be. People who ate here had lots of money, but the facade looked like a run-down old brick house. The sisters arrived at the restaurant and were seated inside, only to discover that the studio honchos who were supposed to dine with them were running late.

"LA traffic, you know," the waiter commented reflexively.

Actually, they didn't know. They had grown up in Oakley, where a traffic jam meant one of the Tucker brothers was driving a tractor through town. Those Tucker boys had a reputation. And a way with the Riley women. Both Kiley's boyfriend, Josh, and their older sister Jane's husband, Wade, were both Tuckers. There were no unattached Tucker men left for Miley to claim, not that any of them had ever been her type anyway. Even Evan, the head of the family and number one supporter of the town of Oakley, had found true love with Jane's friend Donna, who was now almost more of a mother-figure to her. Although, Miley could not deny that she had crushed on Wade back when she was a teenager.

Even the larger cities in Alabama that Miley had on occasion held events at were nothing compared to the size of this city. And the energy! Miley could feel her skin buzzing while sitting at this table in the middle of the restaurant. Her complexion could definitely have used a few more tanning visits to fit in. Yes, she was right here in the middle of all the action. Someone famous could walk by any second. She would meet them, maybe get a picture. Maybe some of their fame would rub off on her. Thinking this made her lightheaded.

Or maybe it was the lack of food. Who invites someone halfway across the country and then arrives forty-five minutes late to lunch?

Presently, the movie studio honchos showed up. There were three of them. They looked important in their freshly pressed suits and striped ties. But Miley and Kiley were still in the yoga pants they had left home in. They hadn't even been to their hotel yet to freshen up. They stood up as the men approached.

"Ah, Miss Riley. It is so good to have you with us here in LA for the production of our movie."

Miley noticed they didn't refer to it as Kiley's book, they only mentioned it as "our movie." The lead guy shook Miley's hand first. Miley and Kiley exchanged a look, but went with it.

"And this must be your lovely sister, Miley," the man then turned and took Kiley's hand. Miley rolled her eyes. Lovely sister? What a load of B.S. They were identical, obviously, since this guy already couldn't tell them apart. This kind of mix up hadn't happened in years, because Kiley's former jet black hair had made such a striking difference in their appearances.

"Uh, I am actually K," Kiley informed them. Miley noticed that Kiley didn't offer up her full first name to them, only her pen name. The man apologized for the confusion, but showed no signs of being flustered. It seemed like he and the other men didn't really care who was who. They were only there to put in the required face time to make sure this project went smoothly. Oh, and of course the company-sponsored lunch.

The waiter came and they ordered drinks. What seemed like an eternity later, they ordered appetizers. Miley controlled her hunger and managed to not eat the whole plate herself. But she was very sad to see the waiter remove the platter with food still on it. Their entrees were still nowhere in sight.

Normally, Miley would have ordered something dainty when dining among the stars in Tinseltown. She would have guessed that she would be wearing something fabulous as well. But not having eaten all day and knowing she had the elastic waistband of yoga pants on her side, she ordered the pricey bacon cheeseburger with some sort of exotic cheese on it. Miley wasn't a picky eater. As long as she didn't look too close, she could eat just about anything.

4

Miley and Kiley finally made it back to the hotel. Miley saw one of the famous shield-shaped Beverly Hills street signs along the way. The studio had put the sisters up at the Beverly Hilton. Miley had been hearing the hotel's name on television her entire life, usually at the end of game shows. "Contestants stay at the beautiful Beverly Hilton..." It had been the setting of both the Golden Globes and the Daytime Emmy Awards; also the unfortunate location of Whitney Houston's last breath. The outside of the building was so beautiful, with the sun glinting off all of the balconies and the water cascading in the fountain, it was wealth personified. Miley had to blink back tears once again. The room itself was the very definition of tasteful and classy, with the bedding and curtains in a rich crème and gold pallet on the two double beds. There is no way these colors would ever hide any stains. It was as if the hotel picked the lightest colors possible as a challenge for themselves. The balcony gave a breathtaking view of the Los Angeles skyline.

But the real definition of luxury was the television in the bathroom.

They both wanted a nap more than anything, but instead changed their clothes and headed off to the movie set. Kiley's rental car had been delivered to the hotel. They rode back to the rental car place with the delivery man, then got slightly lost trying to find the studio. The GPS would have helped, but it was stuck in Spanish mode.

The recently formed Plateau Studios probably wasn't as impressive as the larger studios that had been around for a century, but it was still awfully cool to be on an actual movie studio lot, Miley thought. This is where the magic happens! This is how everyday beautiful people, pretending to be other beautiful people, become adored by millions purely by having their image bigger than life on the giant movie screen.

Miley's secret dream was to be a black and white movie star in the 1930s. She could totally picture herself in a long, form-fitting sequined gown, the flash from hundreds of cameras causing the dress to light up the night. Miley would be shining at the center of the attention, her hair platinum blond and rolled in giant curls as big as soup cans. Her lips and fingernails would be as red as blood. Miley would sell her soul to be that glamorous. She had told this to Kiley once, and Kiley had laughed at her. That is why it was now a "secret" dream. Well, that, and Miley didn't own a time machine.

They checked in at the security shack. After some back and forth by the guards on their walkie-talkies, the sisters were told to park in Lot C and someone would meet them there.

As they were closing the car doors a very handsome young man pulled up in a golf cart, an ID badge hanging from his neck. He had blond hair that was spiked in a messy disarray. All the hair product on it sparkled in the afternoon sun. Miley tried to guess his age. His face and actions had a youthful quality, but his charming smile made him at least twenty-one.

"Hey, I heard there were a couple hot twins down here that wanted to see a movie set. I would love to show you the *Bloodbath 3* set, but unfortunately the only set filming today is *Don't Judge a Boy by His Shoes*," the man-boy finished, his eyes twinkling as he stepped off the cart.

"It is so nice to finally meet you in person. We have talked on the phone so many times!" Kiley hugged him. That is when it hit Miley that she knew his face. She had seen it in many an entertainment magazine, usually with her sister's name below it. He was the boy whose shoes were not to be judged.

"OMG, you are Bobby Patterson!" Miley instantly felt her face flush at the realization.

"In the flesh." He held his hands out wide as Kiley climbed onto the front seat of the golf cart on the passenger side. Miley stood there a beat too long gaping at him. When she realized they were waiting for her to get on, she jumped on the back. Bobby sat down and floored it, almost spilling Miley off before she found the posts to grab ahold of behind her seat. Kiley kept up a steady stream of conversation with him in the front.

As she turned in her seat to see where they were headed, the wind created by their speed felt good on Miley's face, hot from embarrassment. She didn't know why she was being so silly. Bobby's looks did nothing for her on the flat, shiny magazine pages. And maybe her nerves would have been unruffled if she had met him on the set, as she had already anticipated in her head. Having him be the one to pick them up was unexpected. She had at first assumed he was merely an intern or a page. Miley felt a bit angry at herself. She had been looking for stars since she had gotten up this morning. Now, when one drives right up to her, she is too dense to even realize it.

That was it. She was going to have to stay on her guard.

They approached a large, unexceptional building. It looked like warehouse, as did all the buildings around it. Bobby drove the golf cart up to the double doors and stopped. He honked the horn. It sounded like the horn for a tiny clown car. A security guard that must have been standing just inside the door opened it, allowing Bobby to drive right in. Bobby and the guard nodded their heads toward each other in acknowledgement.

After driving down a few more gray, concrete block hallways, Bobby beeped again at another door. This time they entered a giant room where one whole wall was green. When they said green screen, they weren't kidding. The color was so bright that it hurt Miley's eyes to look at it. Large props were arranged on the green floor: big rocks, a fake tree, and a bench. It looked like one of those children's play areas at the shopping mall that Miley always imagined were teaming with germs.

"This is my own book, and I have no idea what scene you guys are going to film here," Kiley told Bobby. The golf cart stopped, and they climbed out.

"It is the fight between Chad and Dave," he told them, using the characters' names.

Miley knew from her favorite entertainment industry online database, St★rDirt, that Bobby Patterson's height was six foot four inches. She clearly never thought about how tall that would be in real life standing next to her. His movements were actually a bit lanky, which Miley could see would help him play the younger role very easily.

"I thought they would film that outside. Since, you know, it takes place outside," Kiley responded.

"It's a fight scene. Everything has to be controlled. The floor is padded. The studio can't take a chance on me or Nick getting hurt while filming."

"But the second unit has already shot this scene, right?"

"Yes. But now they need our close-ups," Bobby explained.

"I couldn't have explained the process better myself," a man said as he approached them.

"Hi Jack! So nice to finally meet you in person," Kiley said. "Miley, this is Jack Kahn, the director. We have done a lot of video chats."

"Nice to meet you, Miley." Jack shook her hand. Jack was a thin, middle-aged man with glasses. He wore a ball cap, but nervously took it off and put it back on again so frequently that it was clear to see that it was meant to cover where his scalp had begun to show through his dark hair. Maybe his weight was a result of anxiety as well. He wore roundish glasses that Miley couldn't help but think made him look nerdier than he actually was. He had the appearance of a high school science teacher. But he was a happy guy and smiled a lot. His clothes were wrinkled and too big, hanging off of his small frame, as if he had had a dramatic weight loss, but no time to shop for a new wardrobe.

"You would not believe all the details that are in your sister's head that she neglected to put into her book. If she had put them in the book, the actors wouldn't need me hanging around. I'm gonna send Bobby here off to wardrobe now, so we can shoot the scene sometime today. Help yourselves to the craft services table. Let me know if you have any questions," Jack said.

"Why is it called craft services?" Miley asked.

Jack looked confused, then smiled. Apparently he had only been expecting questions directly about the production.

27

"Uh, I believe because they are providing the 'service' of nourishment to the 'crafts,' such as cameras, sound, props, grips, etc.," he replied.

Miley nodded in comprehension.

When they were sitting by themselves, munching on cinnamon rolls as big as their heads, Miley asked Kiley the question that had been gnawing on her brain for the last twenty minutes.

"How did you get to be so chummy with Bobby Patterson?"

"Oh, well. He just called me to get some deeper insight on his character."

"So, you have been talking to Bobby Patterson on the phone for a few weeks and neglected to tell me?" Miley summarized.

"Mmm. Actually, probably more like a few months," Kiley corrected, gloating.

"So you, like, have his cell number? Do you even realize how huge this is? He could know other actors we could meet. This could TRANSFORM our whole vacation."

"Miley, he's got work to do. I'm not going to bother him."

"He has apparently been calling you up and bothering YOU for months," Miley retorted.

"That is different. He wants to do justice to characters I created. He isn't asking me to hook him up with my sister," Kiley said.

"I have a feeling if he was, I wouldn't get the message," Miley pouted.

"Plus, he is dating Christy anyway." Kiley let that bomb drop on her.

"Oh my God. You mean that the tabloids have it right? Bobby is really dating his co-star?"

"But you didn't hear that from me," Kiley added, sarcastically.

"Wow. I really need to move out here. Everything in my life would be so much more exciting."

"You can't."

"Why?" Miley asked.

"Because I would miss you too much," Kiley replied.

At that moment, Christy walked out casually onto the set. She was made up similarly to Bobby, with hair and makeup designed to take about five years off of her appearance. Her chestnut hair poured in ringlets down her shoulders, in that way it did in movies and never in real life. She headed over to see Jack.

Movies and television shows always try to hire actors over eighteen to play high schoolers. Casting actors who are minors comes with legal filming restrictions, and usually onset tutors as well. Of course, this created a never-ending inferiority complex for each generation of viewers watching at home: boys wondering why their faces were covered in zits and their bodies were still less than five feet tall with no hair, and girls puzzled why plentiful bosoms had yet to sprout.

Miley gawked at Christy as she talked to Jack, gesturing her hands this way and that to different points on the stage. When she finished, Kiley waved her over to them. Miley broke out in a sweat again, not sure why. Her heart pounded loudly in her ears, making it hard to hear. This reaction was so ridiculous, but involuntary.

"Hi Christy. I know that you are busy, but I wanted to introduce my sister, Miley. She will be out here with me for the next two weeks."

"Oh, it is so nice to meet you," she said, shaking Miley's hand.

"Oh, no. It is nice to meet you. I mean, I love the work you did in *Crash My Car*. It is one of my favorite movies. It must be so great to be an actress." Miley was blabbering now.

"Oh, that movie was such a pain to film. The stunt scenes took forever to set up, then the cars never crashed right," Christy responded.

No one spoke now, and Miley knew that she should, but words escaped her. Kiley picked up the slack to ease the awkwardness. "There may be a few fights, but at least there are no car crashes in this one."

"Yes! No one could be happier about that than me. Oops, gotta run. It was nice meeting you," Christy flashed her straightened, whitened smile, then rushed back to where the stage was set up.

"Nice girl, isn't she? The tabloids always try to paint her as some bitch."

"Mmm, hmmm" was all Miley could manage. She loved to play a game to see how close she could come to knowing her favorite celebrities. It was like a mix of the scientific concept of six degrees of separation and the trivial game six degrees of Kevin Bacon. Except in Miley's version, it combined regular people and celebrities to give her the best result. She quickly added Bobby and Christy's names to her list, and recalculated her previous mental flowchart of familiarity.

They sat around and watched the very slow process of filmmaking while filling up on craft services for dinner. When the production wrapped for the day at 11:00PM, they were taken by security back to the appropriate parking lot. Except they did not remember which car was their rental car. They had ridden in it, but neither of them had given the exterior design (or color or make or model) a second glance. Modern technology should have made finding the car as easy as pushing a button; as in, the button on the key fob. But the battery seemed to be dead in it. Either that, or one too many rental customers had abused it.

Kiley tried the key in several of the cars remaining in the parking lot before she found their vehicle. Turned out it was a very nondescript, white, mid-size sedan. The security guard stood by and assured every passerby that they were not thieves, just tourists. While he mostly got a chuckle out of their exploits, he did provide them with help they desperately needed and were very grateful for—he fixed the GPS. As tired as they were, Kiley and Miley never would have found their hotel again in the maze of streets, in the dark, without it.

"Hello?"

"Oh, Trav, I am so tired. But I wanted to make sure to give you a goodnight call, so that you wouldn't feel neglected."

"Miley, you sound like crap."

"I have been up since 5:30AM and traveled halfway across the country."

"You slept on the plane," Kiley yelled obnoxiously in the background.

"Well, I guess then I won't ask you how your flight was. Have you met any stars?"

"Only the future ones in Kiley's movie." Miley paused to yawn. "I am so tired. Goodnight, Trav."

"Goodnight, Miley."

Miley began snoring before the phone disconnected.

5

The next two days Miley and Kiley spent on the movie set. *Don't Judge a Boy by His Shoes* was a modern-day, role-reversal retelling of the classic fairy tale *Cinderella*. They watched scenes being shot, mostly ones set in high school. There were lots of lockers and desks. Miley wanted to see the glamorous mansion that Kiley had described in her book, where the main character, Monica, was supposed to live her extravagantly rich lifestyle. It was supposed to symbolize Prince Charming's castle from the original story. She was disappointed to find out that all the external shooting had already been completed of the house in Beverly Hills. All interior shots would be done on the soundstage.

Miley never found herself wishing for an actual acting career. No, she knew that was a lot of work. She didn't want to be the actress playing the role. She wanted to be the character in the movie living the grand life, never making the wrong decision because the script would never allow for it. It would be like Peter Pan taking her into Neverland, rather than reading it in a book or going on some amusement ride.

Miley spent a lot of time observing the movie crew. She tried to figure out what each of their jobs was by watching them. When there was something she couldn't figure out on her own, she asked them during one of the many breaks between filming that happened as lights and cameras were reset. By the third day, many of them recognized her and greeted her by name.

Miley also watched the actors. They would often come over and ask Kiley how they should play a certain scene in the story, but they didn't say much to Miley, beyond a polite greeting. And Miley herself couldn't think of anything to talk to them about. She found herself realizing that the stars were so very NORMAL. A spotlight didn't follow them around everywhere they went (although paparazzi did). They didn't dress everyday like they were attending an awards show. They didn't draw unnecessary attention to themselves in the way Miley believed she would if she were in their famous shoes. In fact, without makeup, most of them were hard to recognize at all.

A little part of Miley was saddened by this. She had come here for the magic. Now she was realizing the business of Hollywood was only to create the illusion of magic. But that wasn't totally disappointing. Miley could picture herself involved in all this somehow. What was there tying her to Huntington anyway? A little family? They could come visit. A little business? Imagine what Miley could build out here for herself. By HERSELF.

TRAVIS

"Hey, Trav."

"Hey, Miley. What's new with you?"

"I have learned a lot about movie production. With all the work they put into them and people involved, it is amazing any of them make any money," she griped.

"So you discovered that Los Angeles is boring. That means you are ready to come home now?"

"No way."

"Hey, I only let you go on the condition you would be back in two weeks," Travis stated more seriously.

"Funny. You think you are the boss of me."

"Someone needs to be. You lack good judgment," Travis stated.

"I think I will choose to be offended by that," Miley replied. She had worded her reply that way because she knew damn well that it was true.

"I tell you these things because I care," he retorted.

"You only care if I come back because you need friends."

"I care that the bright lights of Hollywood might suck you into a hole you can't get back out of."

"You don't know what you are talking about," Miley said.

"I know exactly what I am talking about. Since Kiley mentioned this trip to you, you have done nothing but fantasize about a Hollywood lifestyle for yourself. You can lie to yourself all you want, but I can see the truth."

"Well, then you can see it is time for me to go to bed. 'Night Trav."

The phone signal across the country disconnected. Travis said a silent prayer that Kiley would keep Miley in line, and knowing that if Miley was determined enough, no one would be able to dissuade her.

MILEY

Travis was a little weird in how he saw the world. Miley always looked at the positive side and went full steam ahead. Travis was more cautious. He would get quiet, just contemplating a decision. It was like he was having a lengthy discussion with the devil on his left shoulder and the angel on the right. That is why his catering business had grown steadily, but slowly. Miley had impressively nurtured Pleasantly Perfect Party Planning – For All Occasions from a stagnant business when Jenny ran it into a powerhouse in only a few years.

Miley felt that their differences in personality helped, rather than hindered, their friendship. And there was something familiar in how she and Travis could relate to each other. She loved knowing he always had her back. Because then, well, she didn't have to be cautious and have her own.

"Do you call Travis EVERY night before you go to bed?" Kiley asked.

"I do," Miley replied. "It helps calm me down and helps me unwind before bed. I decompress by telling him all about my day."

"You just said the same thing using three different verbs... Wow. Most guys wouldn't want to listen to a girl's day, unless they were receiving sexual favors from her." Kiley paused. "Is Travis your boyfriend?"

"Oh, no. Just a boy, who is a friend. I mean a guy," Miley replied.

"So you have noticed that he is a grown man. Do you also realize he is cute, funny, nice, smart, and walks erect?"

"What are you saying?" Miley asked, squinting at her sister.

"I am saying he could make a great boyfriend."

"For who?" Miley flung her hands out at her side.

"YOU!" Kiley exclaimed.

"No! He is just a friend. Don't you have any guys you are just friends with?" Miley posed.

"Well, yes. But they all share parents with my boyfriend."

"It's just not that way with him. I actually kind of get a gay vibe from him."

"Does Travis think he is gay?" Kiley asked.

"No. But he might not want to come to terms with it yet."

"Or maybe what you think is a 'gay vibe' is just that he is a nice guy who doesn't merely want to use you for a free apartment."

"Hey! Leave Sandy out of this," Miley fired back.

"But do you see my point?" Kiley inquired.

"Travis never even goes out with anyone."

"Maybe because he has already found the right one." Kiley arched her eyebrows at Miley, accusingly.

6

Wednesday Miley and Kiley went sightseeing. They packed big, brightly colored beach bags full of snacks and drinks. They put on their "I [heart] LA" baseball hats (spelled out in rhinestones, of course). They even bought maps of the stars houses from a vendor on the street corner. They were reveling in all their tacky, tourist glory. Upon further inspection, Kiley was fairly certain half the celebrities on that map were already dead. No matter, they agreed the map would make a great souvenir. They started off the day, before it got too hot, by climbing aboard one of the buses for the tours of stars homes.

They pointed and giggled and laughed. The only star they saw in the flesh was one from a no longer on the air, but very popular, sitcom. They took lots of pictures of him. Most were of the back of his head, too far away, or both. Back home, no one would even be able to tell that it was him. But Miley knew it was because she had spotted the finger on his right hand that was short a tip. She instantly added him into her mental network of six degrees of separation, although she had not actually gotten to converse with him. Her network was expanding quickly. Not quick enough though.

They got back into the rental car and drove around. At first they couldn't find anywhere to go or anything to do. They were driving through cute little suburbs with matching houses and no trees. Then they happened into the edge of the scary part of town. Eventually they stumbled upon the Santa Monica Pier. They rode the historic carousel. They ate lunch there and got smoothies, because that seemed like a very "California" drink; although they actually bought smoothies at the mall at home all the time. But these were "vacation smoothies." So they tasted better, more genuine. And everyone knows food you consume on vacation has fewer calories.

They shopped a little, but mostly browsed. They asked for directions to Paramount Studios and the Hollywood sign. They took the tour at Paramount. They took tons of pictures. They drove out to Griffith Park Observatory and took pictures at sunset of the giant letters that stand sentinel over the city. They went back to their hotel room, put on their PJs, and ordered a pizza from room service while uploading photos to social media. They busted out the super-soft hotel slippers that were in the bathroom.

The pizza was much smaller than they had anticipated for the price. They gave up on room service and ordered pizza to be delivered from the outside. They picked out a movie to watch on pay-per-view while they waited.

A knock finally sounded at the door.

"I'll get it," Kiley called.

"I'll make sure it has the right toppings before he leaves. I'm still hungry and don't want any more delays."

"Yes, master," she hollered back to Miley, already pulling the door open to face the pizza delivery guy. He looked as though he was a college student.

"Hey, you guys order a—," he paused to look at the slip on the cardboard box, trying to read through the grease spots, "meat lover's with mozzi sticks?"

"Yes, that's us," Kiley confirmed. She passed the boxes behind her to Miley. "We ordered a pizza from room service, but when it arrived it was tiny," she added.

"Ya, that is not the first time I have heard that while delivering here," he agreed, handing her a credit card receipt and pen to sign it with. He looked them both over, then began, "Hey, I gotta ask. You guys aren't from around here. Alabama?"

"Yes, how did you know?" Miley asked, opening the box to inspect the order.

"Your accents. My mom's family is from Alabama. My grandmother still lives there. I used to go visit her for a few weeks every summer. Beautiful countryside."

"Oh, yes. Very different from out here," Kiley replied, handing him back the signed receipt.

"Well, I'm used to it here. But there was nothing like hearing the screen door slam against the wooden casing, to fall asleep with the sound of the insects roaring outside the window... Plus, my grandma made the greatest sweet tea. I can almost taste it right now."

"Ya, I bet you can't get a good glass of that around here," Kiley retorted.

"You got that right," he answered.

"You could get a job as tourism ambassador for our state."

"Would probably pay better than pizza delivery. I gotta run. Nice catchin' up with y'all," he drawled to prove he could, and gave them a parting wink. Kiley closed the door and locked the deadbolt behind him.

"Man, now he made me all homesick," Miley said, as she plated up the pizza and breadsticks.

"I know, right. I can't believe I'm gonna say this, but I actually miss the farm."

"Even the dirt and smells?"

"Even the dirt and smells. And especially Josh."

"Hey, at least we got like three times the pizza for the same price we paid for room service," Miley quipped.

Miley didn't need to call Travis that night. He could see what she had posted online. It was like a digital slide show of her day.

TRAVIS

"We should hang like this more often, bro. It seems like you are always either working or hanging out with Miley."

"It seems like that because that IS my life right now," Travis replied, shoving another French fry in his mouth as something on the television screen blew up. "But it will all be worth it someday when I have my own restaurant."

"That doesn't explain Miley."

"She is just a friend."

"Ya, and you are as transparent as the plastic wrap you buy in bulk." Austin continued, gesturing to the TV, "See, this right here. This is great. We need more bro time like this."

"Some of us have to work for a living."

"Hey, I work!"

"Ya, at your father's office, where you can come and go all day as you please." Austin had always been Travis's good friend. They had spent many hours riding skateboards, and then motorcycles together. Austin went to college while Travis worked on his catering business. He thought that Austin sometimes forgot that he was no longer a freewheeling kid in college. Austin still thought life should be one big party. He didn't understand that other young adults actually had responsibilities and obligations. Not everyone was on their parents' payroll.

"You work for yourself. If you want to take a day off, just do it."

"Yes, but then when my rent comes due, it won't seem like such a good idea," Travis replied pointedly.

"I'm saying you need to find more time to hang out."

"But the only reason we are having movie night right now is because Miley is out of town."

"You need to get out, meet some other women. You got that whole emo thing or whatever going on. Chicks dig that."

Travis shook his head. "I don't think so."

"Man, that chick has you wrapped around her little finger. You know she is why you can't get any dates. You already look like you are 'unavailable,' " Austin said, waving his fast food burger towards Travis.

"Maybe I don't want to go out on any dates."

"Ack, man. She has you so whipped."

"I'm sorry if you like playing the field. That's not me," Travis replied, hoping they could depart this topic now.

"If you are going to spend so much time with her, get it over with! Have the sex!" Austin shouted.

"Maybe. Someday."

"Gah!" Austin threw a pillow at Travis's head. "I swear that you just grew a uterus."

Travis was well aware that he had entered the friend zone with Miley many years ago. He was cognizant that she did not see him as a potential boyfriend. He could only hope that something might happen to change her mind about him. And he hadn't had many chances for that in the past three years. That is how long that no-good loser slime ball Sandy had been shacking up with her. When Travis had helped her move her stuff into her new two bedroom apartment, a part of him was very hopeful that he would end up in that other bedroom, evicting her obscene amount of shoes.

But Sandy had conveniently needed a place to stay only a few weeks later. It was such optimal timing that Travis couldn't help but think Miley had had it in mind all along. Travis had never stood a chance. And even when they weren't technically together, Sandy was always there, nearby, spoiling Travis's chances with her. And now, just when Sandy had moved out of the picture, Miley was thousands of miles away.

Austin didn't understand. He changed girls like other people changed underwear. Although, as he often boasted, Austin rarely wore any. Travis was outgoing, but not when it came to women. He didn't have much to offer. Austin was always throwing his father's name and money around. Travis had a fledging business, a tiny apartment, and a crabby-ass mother he wouldn't want to bring any girl home to. And Miley had been all he had wanted since he had met her. He just hoped one day he could be enough for her.

7

MILEY

Thursday they once again lost the sun as they reentered the land of the giant soundstage. The shooting schedule had to be changed. The studio executives were concerned that the budget of the movie was ballooning. They wanted to see a rough reel of scenes and daily shots so far. If the shooting budget was growing, the director explained, then they were seriously considering cutting the marketing budget altogether. No marketing budget meant in that today's terms, the film had no way of ever being a success. There would be no money for MEtube commercials. There would be no money to put the characters' images on boxes of toasted pastries or packages of gum.

Jack was all in a tizzy. This meant they had to have at least a day's worth of shooting the prom scene because it was pivotal to the overall flow of the movie, which hadn't been on the shooting schedule for another two weeks. The studio heads wanted the mock up by Saturday at noon. No shooting would take place on Friday, as Jack would be holed up in a backroom editing suite somewhere with the editors trying to make an unfinished film look worthy of the studios' time and money. Everyone was flustered and running around like chickens with their heads cut off. It didn't help that Jack usually was the gravitational center that everyone else revolved around, and now he himself was spinning out of orbit. Gray stubble had sprouted out about his chin.

The screenwriters were busy completing last minute script tweaks that they previously had had two more weeks to take care of. The script runners were busy running the revised scripts to the actors. The actors and the costume designers were busy doing final touches and alterations on the prom outfits, deciding which elements would simply take too much time and would have to be abandoned. The set designers were doing the same thing. The lighting and sound guys had to wait for all the changes to be made so that they could map out their own locations. Miley even helped with a few of the decorations and floral arrangements. Not that she had ever had any formal training at it, but she had supervised enough weddings to know a tight arrangement from a sloppy one.

"Hey, Travis," Miley cooed into her phone.

"What up?"

"I think I have been on this soundstage for an eternity. How about you?"

"I had an event tonight. Just driving back now," Travis replied from the catering truck.

"I miss your baked herb-crusted chicken."

"I thought you said craft services was 'da bomb'? And that is a direct quote."

"It is, but I think it is making me fat. And my pores are clogging. I miss our Wednesday night dinner and movie together."

"Yes, I had to do it without you. Austin came over instead," Travis said dismissively.

"Aw, what did you do?" Miley asked.

"MacRonnell's and Die Hard."

"Oh, now I am not so jealous," she sneered.

"C'mon. You know you miss cuddling with me on the couch."

"I do. I hope Austin was a suitable replacement."

"Funny," he replied snarkily.

They shot till 3:00AM. Miley and Kiley were exhausted, and, for the most part, they had only watched everyone else work. They fell into bed like two rocks.

8

On Friday, Miley and Kiley slept late. Since half the day was already behind them, they decided to use the rest of the day for relaxation. There was a spa downstairs in the hotel, so they made appointments. The earliest available openings were after lunch.

Since they had time to kill, they went to the pool. They went swimming, sat in the hot tub, and laid in the sun. Kiley pulled out her laptop and moved into the shade in order to be better able to see the screen. She was working on catching up on her emails. Miley was glad her work did not follow her on vacation. This made her remember Travis back home, all lonely because he had no one to play with. Her heart hummed in her chest when she thought of him, as if a bee had stung her heart, causing it to pump toxin through her blood stream, heating up all her vessels and veins.

At their appointed time, they headed into the spa. They got manicures, pedicures, facials, and massages. Miley could not convince Kiley to participate in anymore girlie activities than that.

"Kiley," Miley began.

"Mmm" was her reply as she studied her computer in their hotel room, now with fancy metallic violet fingernails typing away at the keys.

"Do you think I'm organized?"

"Mmm, ya. It is one of your best qualities." There was a pause.

"Kiley, do you think I organize others well?"

"Sure. That is your job," Kiley responded.

"So you think that I could translate those skills into other lines of work?"

"Sure."

"Could I wear an elephant as a hat?"

"No. And you don't have to test me. I am listening to you." There is a long pause.

"I was thinking, that maybe, you know, I might make a good personal assistant to a celebrity."

"Maybe. But there aren't any celebrities in Huntington," Kiley said. There was a pause. "Miley, you aren't seriously considering moving out here, are you?" she asked.

"The thought had crossed my mind."

"But what about your business?"

"Other people change careers all the time. Why can't I?" Miley surmised.

"Most people go from working at a burger joint to the factory. They don't abandon a successful business to play with movie stars."

"It would be like a dream come true though. But I guess that isn't something you would understand. You, wanting to become a writer and all…"

"I understand. I don't want you to do anything hasty that you will later regret."

"I'm a big girl, K. You are the little sister. I am supposed to be the one who gives YOU advice."

Kiley threw up her hands. "OK, backing off," she said. Usually Kiley was not one to give up so easily. She must be hoping to broker an extended period of harmony on this vacation.

Jane's and Kiley's lives always seemed to run so smoothly. They knew what they wanted to do in life. They took the college path. Jane did have that whole being adopted thing to deal with. Miley had to admit that was a challenge she was glad she would never have to experience. But both her sisters found true love with the first (or second) boy they had ever been with. By comparison, Miley's life looked like a train wreck.

Miley had forgone college to hold a succession of mediocre jobs that she wasn't good at, until Jenny took her under her wing. Sure, Miley had helped to grow that business and make it her own. But in the meantime she had had the on-again off-again live-in boyfriend disaster known as Sandy. That was the worst kind. Talk about dysfunctional. When they were off-again, she had to watch him parade his new pop-tarts through there. Miley would try to bring home her own suitors. Sometimes as serious prospects, sometimes solely to make Sandy jealous. Either way, they always ended badly. And much of that time she was lying to her mother about Sandy, leading her to believe that he was actually a female roommate. Maybe it was time for her to take her life into her own hands... and fly.

9

"Where are we going tonight? I want to go to a fancy club and scope for guys!" Miley's exclamation turning into a high-pitched whine.

"God, Miley. It's only 9:00AM. I am trying to enjoy sleeping in and you are already on me about clubbing?" Kiley covered her head with the blankets.

"C'mon, c'mon, c'mon! I've been a very good girl this trip."

"Yes, you have. But I don't need to find a guy. I have one waiting for me at home. Besides, do you really think they are going to let a couple of 'Bama bumpkins like us into a fancy LA club?" Kiley tried to reason with her sister.

"They will if we go shopping this afternoon on Rodeo Drive!"

"I can't believe you actually just squealed at the end of that statement."

"Please-please-please!"

"Alright. Sheesh." Kiley rolled over to the bedside table. "I gotta check my schedule... Well, Rodeo Drive I could do, but not the club. I have a book signing for *Sister Lost* tonight at Chandler's. It is one of the most popular bookstores in LA. It is a big deal to get to make an appearance there. I'm sorry, sis. Maybe tomorrow night."

"But tonight is Saturday night! Everyone knows that is the BEST night to go out," Miley fretted.

"Sorry. Let me get a shower, and then we can shop till I drop," Kiley said, her voice sounding less than enthusiastic. She picked some clothes out of her suitcase, then went into the bathroom and shut the door.

Miley pouted. She decided to channel her negative energy and give Travis a call. He picked up on the second ring.

"Hey baby, how you doin'?"

"Do you always answer the phone like that?" she asked.

"Just for my favorite people."

"Aw, thanks. You always know how to make me feel better."

"What's wrong?" Travis asked, sounding concerned.

"Kiley won't go to a club with me."

"Oh, that doesn't sound like Kiley."

"She has some stupid book signing thing to go to."

"Why don't you go to that with her?" he hedged.

"I have before. They are boring if you are not the person everyone is lined up to see."

"Sounds like a case of sour grapes to me."

"More like a whole vineyard," Miley replied.

"You are in Hollywood! That's always been your dream. And now you are STILL unhappy?"

"I'm high maintenance. You know that."

"That's part of what I love about you," he said, his voice sounding genuine.

"Ha-ha," she laughed it off. "How is everything back home?"

"Same old, same old. I gotta take off soon for the birthday party Jenny is running while you are on vaca."

"Is she doing OK with all that by herself?"

"Oh, yes. Remember, she is the one who trained you," Travis said.

"I worry about her doing it all on her own. You know how I like to be in control of everything."

"I am sure she will cross the t's and dot the i's. Don't worry about what is going on here. Except for me being lonely without you."

"Oh, you will find some way to occupy your time. Probably with those online games you play on your phone."

"You caught me. You should enjoy your vacation while it lasts," Travis stated.

"You know what, you are totally right! I should enjoy my vacation."

"Good. I'm glad I could talk some sense into you."

"You sure did. I am going to go clubbing tonight on my own," Miley stated confidently.

"OK—whoa, wait up. I didn't mean for you to go by yourself—"

"Nope, it is the only logical solution. Oh my God! I can't wait. It is going to be so fun!"

"No, Miley, seriously now. You cannot go to an LA club on your own. People get shot at those places. They OD!"

"Only the famous ones. I'll call you when I get back to my room tonight. IF I do. Later."

She pushed the end button, knowing that Travis was still talking. Miley knew she would never beat him at this argument. There was only one thing to do. She turned her phone off, knowing that he would keep calling to try to talk her out of going to the club all day long. She knew she was being childish. Miley didn't care.

Miley and Kiley headed to Beverly Hills. They hit what seemed like every store on Rodeo Drive—big and small. Miley quickly bought a new outfit and changed into it. She didn't like the looks and service she was getting in these high-end stores in her usual clothes, purchased at the Huntington Square Mall. Kiley didn't care about such things, so clerks still gave her the glare of a potential shoplifter and fashion victim.

Kiley bought one new outfit for her signing tonight. It had silver chains hanging off of it. Kiley did always go more for the edgy look. She also bought a fancy pair of sandals and several accessories: a pair of sunglasses, jewelry, and a black dress hat. Kiley complained that the prices of the clothes were too high.

Miley let her eyes do the shopping. She had paid off her credit cards in anticipation of this trip, and now she was going to make it count. She ignored the judgmental looks of her younger sister, which was difficult. They had the same face. Miley knew Kiley's face today would be her own in the mirror when the bill arrived a month from now. But this was her chance to purchase fine clothes from an actual store, not only off the Internet. There wouldn't be any of the hassle of shipping an item back when it didn't fit. Although, Miley had eaten so much in the past week, she felt like she may have gained a size.

While she purchased many fashionable outfits, she didn't find the perfect club dress until the very last store. As Kiley was nagging her that they had to get a move on or she would be late to her own signing, Miley decided to try on the dress just one size smaller. It was an electric blue number. It was simple, but the belt she bought to wear with it would accentuate it perfectly. It had large interlocking silver circles which, were so big, they went most of the way from her breast to her hip. Her assets weren't large, but the smaller dress size emphasized them nicely. It had short sleeves; so short, you could almost consider them wide straps. It had a low neckline that showed off all of her limited cleavage. The hemline crossed the top of her thighs, playing up her already long legs. With some heavy eye makeup and a daring 'do, she would rock the place tonight.

It didn't matter to Miley that she still didn't have a specific destination in mind.

They got back to the hotel. Kiley quickly started removing tags from her clothes so that she could throw them on for her book signing. In the middle of doing that, her agent called to inquire if she was on her way. Even with all those distractions, Kiley still had time to interrogate Miley on her activities.

"So, what are you going to do tonight?"

"Oh, I haven't decided yet," Miley answered.

"You can still come with me, you know. It is a big book store. I am sure you could find something to buy."

"I could stay in, maybe..." Miley tried to play her sister, which never worked.

Kiley noticed her sister clipping the tags off the electric blue dress and the belt a few minutes later.

"Are you thinking you might go out tonight?" she questioned.

"Maybe. I haven't decided," Miley said in a casual tone. Then added, "I'm not sure I'm done shopping yet."

"Oh, OK. Just be careful. Los Angeles is a much bigger city with much more crime than Huntington."

"Alright, mom," Miley replied.

"Maybe you should stay-in and call Travis. I haven't seen you text him all day. I bet he is very lonely."

Stupid Kiley and her writer's gift for observing details, Miley thought. "Thanks for reminding me. My battery died and

I need to plug it in," she fibbed, but made no move toward the charger on the bedside table.

"You aren't thinking about going clubbing by yourself, are you?"

"I told you. I am still undecided," Miley replied.

"Well, whatever you decide to do, be careful, alright. If I show up back in Alabama with you and your body has a bullet wound or track marks, Mom would never forgive me," Kiley said.

"No, she wouldn't, because she told me to take care of you while we were out here, not the other way around."

Her attempts at playing most responsible sister were thwarted by Miley playing the older sister card. It trumped Kiley, the baby in the family, every time.

"Bye!" Kiley yelled as she grabbed her overstuffed bag and breezed out the door, obligations winning out over the need to babysit a twenty-five-year-old.

Miley went to the hotel phone on the bedside table and dialed the concierge. She asked her what was the best club in town to go to. The woman gave her a few suggestions, but Miley picked up on a name that she knew the stars were known to frequent: The Blue Diamond. She immediately headed into the bathroom to begin getting ready.

10

Miley climbed out of the cab (a cab, because Kiley had taken the rental car) onto the concrete curb of THE Sunset Strip, reaching back in to hand the driver several bills. As she watched the cab pull away, she realized she probably should have put the number for the cab company in her phone. The concierge had placed the call for her from the hotel. This wasn't New York City (not that she had ever actually been there). Taxies driving by were a much rarer sight here. And when you did see one driving, it probably already had a fare, or was on its way to picking one up. But tonight was about spontaneity, although actually she had been planning it since her eyes first popped open this morning.

Miley strutted up the sidewalk to the club, hoping she wouldn't be mistaken for a street walker. She had her dark blond with blonder highlighted locks curled and piled on top of her head, which gave her slightly taller than average frame some added height. The silver high heels she was sporting also helped with the illusion. She had on heavy evening eye makeup, in a shade of blue to match her dress, with silver accents. She was considering making them her signature colors, although she was fairly certain she would never find another occasion to wear this particular dress again once she returned home.

Miley could feel the form-fitting dress inch up her thighs with every stride down the sidewalk, but she was now approaching the club, so she made no move to correct the issue. There was a long line of people standing outside, waiting for the doorman to deem them cool enough to enter.

They would be standing there all night.

Miley was positive lining up like cattle would not be the means for her to get in. Luckily, she had come prepared for such an occasion.

Miley confidently walked toward the entrance. She stopped behind the first paparazzo she came to near the door, but closest to the street. She put her hand on his shoulder, out of sight of the doorman. This immediately got his attention. She leaned in very close to speak right in his ear.

"Take a few pictures of me, would you please?" She used her baby doll voice that always worked on Travis when she wanted something. At the same time, she grabbed his hand that was not holding a camera and slipped a crisp fifty dollar bill into it. It might seem like an expensive way to get attention, but she knew she wouldn't have to buy herself any drinks all night the way she looked. It seemed like a fair trade off in her book.

Miley spun out from behind him and said a silent prayer that he would take the bait.

He did.

"Over here!" the photographer yelled, and Miley faced him, did a little pose, and broke out her biggest smile. With a plane ticket, a very expensive dress, and a bribe, she had made a lifelong dream a reality. But she wasn't stopping here. Oh no. If she was going to push the limits, she was going all the way.

As they took the bait, the other paparazzi started snapping photos of her. It was working! They all simply assumed she was a star that the other photographers must be more familiar with than they were. She had played a head game on them all. She had watched enough OMGz to know that the photogs sometimes mistakenly took pics of non-famous people, only to sort it out later. But Miley only needed it to work for sixty seconds.

She spun toward them, making her way up the sidewalk tight with photographers, to the door. Her heart beat overtime. She made the mistake of pausing and actually looking at the bouncer. This gave her away as being a total non-celebrity average Jane. The bouncer, a large, imposing African-American man who must have weighed three hundred pounds, raised an eyebrow at her.

Oh God, the jig was up!

Then he looked sideways to where a couple of girls in dayglo spandex and Bumpits were bickering with the doorman and his list. With a nod of the head so slight that Miley was not sure she had even seen it, the bouncer pulled the door open just enough for her to squeeze in. And with that, her faithful public was forgotten.

Miley wandered around upon first entering the club, feeling a little bit lost. It was a lot like she had seen on TV shows and how she expected it to be. Multi-colored laser lights were bouncing around the room. Strobe lights reflected off a disco ball. A DJ was spinning on stage.

What she wasn't prepared for was that being in the middle of all that sensory overload was much different than watching it on a television screen on your couch. It was easily ten times as overwhelming as the flashing lights and noise of any casino she had been in. The bass drowned out any other sounds. It was as if the music was actually playing inside her eardrums. It seemed like it was even making her silver dangly earrings bounce. The darkness made it hard to see until the lasers flashed nearby, then she was temporarily blinded. The whole place smelled like some wonky brand of incense.

Miley got braver and slowly walked around the room, getting the lay of the land. It really wasn't as big as she had originally thought by her temporary blindness. It still being early, the dance floor was not packed by any means. The walls were painted a blue so dark, it was almost purple. She went into the restroom to check her makeup. There was only one unisex room with several stalls. A girl with long, white-blond hair who didn't even look old enough to have gotten into the club legally was at the sink, snorting cocaine. Sounds that were most likely a couple having sex were coming from one of the stalls.

"Want a hit? You look like you could use it," the girl asked Miley.

"No, I'm good. I haven't started drinking yet," Miley replied. She inwardly cursed herself for letting her internal worries show outwardly.

"The way you look, you won't have any trouble getting drinks tonight." The girl pushed back her hair that had been carefully styled to look as though she had just rolled out of bed.

"Thanks," Miley said. The compliment was just the boost her confidence needed.

"You here by yourself?" The blond gave her a sideways glance.

"Yes. I'm not into chicks, though."

"My friend Mark will be here later," she continued on, unfazed. "You should meet him."

"That sounds great," Miley said, not knowing anything about Mark, and doubting she would ever see this girl again.

"See you later," Miley called, heading back out into the club.

"Later," the girl said. Miley wished she had thought to go with the shorter, one word farewell. It gave a much more polished impression to strangers.

Upon exiting the restrooms, Miley saw that the club was in fact as large as she had first thought. Near the bar was a doorway that led into a private back room. Frosted glass doors blocked it off from the main dance floor area. Miley made a move for the door, but then stopped. She could barely make out the silhouettes of two bulky body guards, one on either side of the door. Miley felt her heart and excitement level drop. So, that was where the VIPs hung out. That meant it was highly unlikely Miley would bump into a celebrity on the dance floor.

Miley went and took a seat at the bar to drown away her sorrows. The bartender brought Miley her first drink, no charge. It was from a female. Well, if Miley felt like switching teams, it could be her lucky night.

Miley had been on the floor dancing with strange men all night. Some were polite. Some groped her, but she was too inebriated to care. She took a break and sat for a minute at the bar, but sitting reminded her that she needed to pee. Alcohol always went right through her.

She made her way back to the restroom. While washing her hands, she got a fit of giggles.

"Well, there you are! And it looks like you are having a good time." It was the blond girl, from earlier.

"We have to stop meeting like this," Miley gestured to the quickly deteriorating hygiene of the high traffic bathroom.

"I didn't get your name earlier..."

"Miley."

"Miley, huh? I'm June, short for Juniper. I know, my parents were hippies." She rolled her eyes. "I love your accent. Is it real or for a role?"

"Oh, real. I'm from Alabama."

"Alabama? What brings you all the way out here?"

"I came with my sister. Maybe you have heard of her—K. Riley, wrote *Don't Judge A Boy By His Shoes*. It's being made into a movie." Miley knew that tomorrow she would die with envy that she had name-dropped her own sister at a fancy Los Angeles club. But she craved acceptance into Hollywood's inner circle, and tonight she would do anything to get it.

"I am trying to 'break in,' so they say. So far, I've had all of the bad luck and none of the good. You could say I am just broke."

Miley giggled a little too loudly at the statement that really wasn't meant to be a joke.

"Hey, my friend Mark is here now. C'mon."

With that, the dainty little pale waif June pulled Miley out of the restroom doorway so quickly that Miley, who was a good five inches taller, almost fell.

June pulled Miley right over to the frosted glass doors.

June pulled her through the frosted glass doors.

THE FORBIDDEN DOORS.

It was very smoky in the back. Which was funny, because Miley was fairly certain there were laws against smoking in bars. It seemed just one of the freedoms that fame awarded. She would love to discover more benefits. June towed Miley through the smoke to what must have been the very rear table.

"Miley, I'd like for you to meet my posse. This is Ryan and Jackson, Charlotte and Ray, Michael, and Mark," June said.

Miley could see that Ryan and Jackson and Charlotte and Ray seemed to be couples. Michael nodded when he heard his name, but never even looked up from his phone. As her eyes reached the last face, the man spoke.

"June, really. You know it is MY posse."

THIS was June's friend Mark?

Mark Tennyson.

MARK TENNYSON!

Mark Tennyson that some people believed could be the next Tom Cruise?! He was considered one of the top young hot stars in Hollywood to not yet have his big starring role. He made all the Top 25 under 25 lists. He was twenty-four years old.

Miley's head was filled with punctuation. She wondered if that is how Kiley's head was all the time.

"Of course it is! Mark Tennyson. It is so great to meet you!" Miley gushed.

"Finally, an appropriate response tonight. I was starting to feel like a has-been."

"That is because Miley is from out of town," June chimed in.

"I can hear that for myself," Mark stated curtly. If she had been sober, Miley might have found his reply rude toward June. But in her current drunken, star-struck state, she found it assertive and a turn on.

Miley thought she might lose her mind! Here she was, in a fabulous dress, hanging in a cool club, with one of the hottest male stars in Hollywood. She felt like she was in a dream. Now her vacation had truly begun.

He had jet black hair. The leather jacket he wore matched it. His hair was longer now than Miley had ever seen it in the movies. He had it held back with gel, which made it glisten, even in this dim light. His eyes were dark pools, hard, as if they were frozen black ice in winter; like a bird's eyes. He had a strong jawline.

Mark had perfectly straight teeth and perfectly sculpted eyebrows—all work done professionally, Miley would surmise. Still, his natural features were striking. It was as if he was born to be an actor. Even in this town of beautiful people, Mark's features glowed, as if stone carved by God and kissed by an angel. He looked like old Hollywood royalty sitting there. He could have been a black and white star time-traveled to the present. His handsomeness was timeless. Mark fit right into Miley's 1930s Hollywood fantasy.

Miley wanted so badly to sit next to him, as no one else was on that end of the booth. But something in his stare told Miley to proceed with caution. It seemed she would have to win some sort of cool test with him first to be worthy. June must have already been familiar with this behavior, as she stood by Miley and made no move to sit either.

"Miley's in town because her sister wrote the book that the shoe boy movie is based on. They are here to watch the filming," June said, bumping Miley in the arm to move her forward.

"Ah, so you do have a Hollywood connection after all. I was beginning to think that June was bringing me strays off the street," Mark quipped.

"Ha-ha," June replied, forcefully pushing Miley over into the spot next to Mark, and then squeezed herself in on the end. Mark put his arm around Miley's shoulders. He sat there with both his arms outstretched, laying along the back of the booth, a cigarette in one hand, a drink in the other.

She tried to slyly turn her head to look at him, to study him so close, without being too obvious about it. But he sensed her gaze and turned toward her. She became lost in those dark pools of mystery, and she thought he was going to kiss her. But instead he just smiled at her. In a way, it was much more hypnotizing. As his smile enchanted her, smoke leaked out between his luminescent teeth. Miley felt like she was in the presence of a dragon. It would not be the only time she felt that way tonight.

June, on Miley's left, was very loud, often shouting over Miley to be heard by the others in the party. But Miley couldn't be upset with her. June was the one who had introduced her to this wonderful spot in the world. Miley no longer had to envy— she was now the envy of others.

Miley felt such attraction for Mark, and she didn't understand why. He wasn't even her type. Her type was scrawnier, with merely a few well-placed muscles. And blond hair. She liked blonds with blue eyes. It may have been formed from watching too many *Dukes of Hazzard* episodes with John Schneider when she was a little girl. Her dad loved that TV show.

Mark ordered more drinks for the table. Miley got a cosmopolitan. Mark asked her about her sister's movie, like he cared. Like he cared!

"So, Jack Kahn is directing that pic, right?" Mark said in his sexy voice. Miley could imagine nothing that sounded sweeter.

"Oh ya, he is a very nice guy."

"So you've met him then?" Mark led.

"Yes. He was freaking out last time I saw him because some big sample reel thing was due to the studio today."

"Oh really."

"Yes. It caused a big scuttlebutt on the set. Everyone rushing around, doing stuff last minute."

"You don't say." Mark added his current cigarette to the overloaded ashtray for it to burn itself out. He lit another, then offered one to Miley. She wasn't usually a smoker. Usually she wasn't a heavy drinker either, but she was tonight. She took the cigarette he handed her and held it to her lips. He let her light it off of his. It was a very intimate gesture, lingering inside his personal space.

"I even had to pitch in. I helped with set design." She added it about two minutes too late to still be part of the conversation. But she still felt it was important. She wanted to give the impression that she was not just a tourist. She could be part of the movie-making machine too, even if it was not in a role as glamorous as actor.

"They must have loved that," Mark said, smiling sweetly to her, even leaning toward her, as if to hear her better. Her lust boiled under the surface. She couldn't stop picturing Mark having her bent over this dirty table, her electric blue dress hiked up around her waist as he nailed her from behind. She could picture him thrusting into her, over and over again. He would have sweat on his forehead, but not a perfectly-gelled hair out of place. She would be so tight he would moan in ecstasy.

Miley found herself getting wet at the fantasy, which flashed through her mind in mere seconds.

Then it happened.

Mark Tennyson kissed her. And not like a polite, nice-to-meet-you kiss. His tongue was in her mouth and foraging for gold. Miley's muscles fluttered deep within her abdomen.

"You are a great kisser," Miley said a few minutes later, when he broke the kiss to light another cigarette. She sensed her words were slurred.

"You are not so bad yourself," Mark replied.

Miley took a quick peek to see if June had noticed, but June's high seemed to have worn off. She could only manage a bored stare into the rest of the smoke-filled room. Miley wondered when was the last time that June had slept.

"Have you seen the Hollywood sign?"

"Yes. I took a million pictures. Like all the dorky tourists do, I guess..."

"But you aren't simply a tourist." He seemed to have trouble spitting out the word. "You have a personal connection to a hot studio property."

"Yes, I guess I do," Miley said, looking into his eyes. They were so dark, she could see her own reflection in them. She was grinning widely at him.

"I can give you something not every tourist gets to experience," Mark said in a voice so sultry, Miley felt like someone had written the line and the stage directions for him. She swallowed. His next words contained no surprise. "I can fuck you by the light of Hollywood sign at night." Mark held her gaze, daring her to accept.

"You drive," Miley managed to say, and sound like she was demanding that he be in control. It was a great technique to cover up that she had no vehicle to drive.

Mark made a move to get up. Miley shrugged to indicate she could go nowhere as long as June was blocking her in. With his hand on her shoulder, Mark gave June an aggressive shove. She looked in his direction, gave him a sour expression, and then stood to let them out.

Oh God! Suddenly Miley was standing next to him. What was she supposed to do now? She felt an A.S.S.: Awkward Social Situation. She was dying to hold his hand, but knew that probably wasn't right. She was surprised at how short he was. Miley was five foot eight inches barefoot, taller tonight in her heels. Mark's eyes didn't meet her own. She was sure IMDb had listed him at a respectable six feet. Mark put his arm around her shoulders, like he was hanging onto her for support. This caused Miley to hunch over a little under his weight.

11

At the frosted doors, one of the bouncers accompanied them through the kitchen and out a back door. The headlights of a very fast-looking black sports car flashed as a "bloop-bloop" sound filled the air in a private parking lot squeezed in between the surrounding structures.

"My baby. I try never to let valet drive her."

Mark went around and jumped into the driver's seat, leaving Miley to let herself into the passenger side.

"Wow, there are so many lights in here, it looks like the Los Angeles skyline." The dashboard was lit up like a Christmas lights display. As Mark tore out onto the street and hit the accelerator, Miley could see her description was apt. "I can't tell where the lights in the car end and the lights of the city begin," Miley exclaimed.

"That's how I like it." Mark smiled a devilish grin, then floored it. They streaked through the city streets during the early morning hours. A misty rain had begun to fall. The wet blacktop reflected the traffic lights that had all turned to flashing amber hours ago. It seemed like they were driving on molten lava; the only way not to burn was to drive fast. Miley wanted to throw her head back and recite that line from *Dirty Dancing*, when Johnny and Baby are in the car together. But Miley could sense that wasn't a side of herself that she should reveal to Mark.

They drove in silence for a while, only listening to the powerful engine purr. Eventually Mark switched on the radio. It was too loud, blaring electronic club-thumping dance beats. It was exactly the type of music the frosted glass doors had mostly blocked out of the VIP room at the club.

Mark stopped the car. Miley looked out the dark-tinted windows to verify that they had indeed made it all the way out here so quickly. The Hollywood sign overlooked the city, but it was actually on the outskirts, on the side of a mountain. The locals seemed to call it a hill.

Mark switched the music to some slow and sexy R&B. He leaned in and kissed Miley again in the same urgent way he had at the club. When they got tired of leaning around the stick shift, he climbed into Miley's seat. There wasn't much room, but they were on top of each other, so it all worked out.

Mark's leather jacket, shirt, and pants were removed, tossed into the driver's seat. Miley's tight dress was shoved up and down, respectively, until it looked like a tube top that only covered her middle. Mark sucked on her nipples until they were raw. He must be a boob man.

Miley had her arm wrapped around the back of his neck. Mark moved his head just enough to look up into Miley's eyes. He gave her a little smile. His black hair was in disarray, having broken free of the hair gel. A lock hung across his forehead and into his eyes. In that moment, he looked younger, more innocent. He reminded her of the boys she had dated back home. Miley's heart fluttered. She had never had feelings this strong for anyone before. He craned his neck up to suck on the hollow of her neck. She let out a soft moan. Her body turned to jelly.

"What do I have to do to get invited back to your place?" Miley might as well put all her cards on the table. She was virtually naked in front of a movie star. Why not find out where she really stood?

"Give me a really good blow job, and you are there" was his reply.

Well, that seemed simple enough. Miley had never gotten an award for her skills in that area, but she had never received any complaints either.

So, she devoured his manhood as if her celebrity stalker card counted on it. And it must have been good, because he pulled her up from under the dashboard, then threw her down onto the seat, and entered her. All the fireworks that had been smoldering in her all night now set off like a bonfire. She couldn't help but climax, over and over again. She bit at his neck and clawed at his back, and he seemed to like it. It seemed to stoke his fire hotter. She could hear his rough panting over her own gasps for air.

They eventually ended up in a sweaty heap in the seat, much as they had been in the act, due to the lack of space.

"Dude, I think we jacked up your seat." Miley was worried how he would react.

"No problem. The exterior and the engine are the important parts to take care of. When I sell this car, the more jizz that is in the car, the greater my legend will be." Mark's words were dripping with his big ego.

12

"I'm going to have to ask you to remove your shoes."

"Of course." She removed her spike heels, casting them aside by the front door. Miley hoped this was an indication that Mark wanted her to stay for an extended period of time. She removed the pins from her hair and shook it out, letting it fall around her shoulders. She hoped it had the desired effect on him. Mark's cigarette smoke from the club and the drive clung to it, invading her nose. Kneading her toes into the plush white carpet, she flashed him a ready smile. Miley had always seen herself as special, but now she had actual celebrity confirmation that she was.

They moved through the entry way into the living room. The vertical space extended all the way up to the second story, with large ceiling fans lazily spinning at an ineffective speed. The furniture was all in neutral colors, blending into the room, as she was sure it was meant to. What really grabbed her attention was the wall of windows that overlooked the dimly lit pool and the woods beyond. This house didn't have an ocean view, something she was sure would be remedied after he had a few more starring roles on his resume. Across the room were shiny wooden stairs leading up to the second story rooms. Mark led her back to the kitchen, featuring a huge island and stainless steel appliances. They passed an unlit fireplace centrally located between the lounging and eating spaces. Miley couldn't help but think it would make an excellent spot for cuddling on a cool evening. He took her through his home gym, also overlooking the pool, and the home theater, devoid of windows. The possibilities of Mark in a private dark room flashed in her brain.

"Wow, this is seriously a fantastic house," Miley complimented him.

"Well, you haven't even seen the best room yet."

"Oh ya? And what is that? Wine cellar? Cigar humidor?"

"No, but those are great suggestions for when I upgrade." He opened the double mahogany doors in front of them, and motioned for Miley to enter. "The master bedroom." A low glow materialized in the room, a motion sensor activating small lamps on either side of the bed. The red shades gave off a crimson glow. They matched the satin sheets on the bed.

"Interior designer?" Miley cocked an eyebrow.

"No, no. This one is all my creation," he boasted. Miley didn't believe a word out of his mouth. But she wrapped her arms around him, making sure to rub her body up against his in her tight blue dress, as she laid a deep kiss on him.

"Mmmm. That's nice."

"Thank you," Miley cooed.

"Did you have a good time in the car?"

"I did. But I am ready for another round."

"How about we make it a little more interesting?" he posed to her.

"Interesting?"

"Well, you asked to come back to my house. And now that we are here, there are certain amenities we have to our advantage."

Miley backed away from him a step. "Now you are scaring me," she said playfully, although she was indeed a little frightened.

"You'll see" were his only words as he reached around her back to seductively unzip her dress. He unlatched her bra, letting her breasts spill out. Miley followed his lead, pushing her dress to the floor. Then she pulled his T-shirt over his head, and proceeded to unbutton his jeans. He pushed them and his boxer briefs down at the same time to expose his ready manhood. She caressed his chest and cock, and then embraced him, making sure to rub her heat against him as their bodies touched.

They kissed, him laying her back down on the bed. He let go of her then, moving to the bedside table between the bed and the window. The coldness of rejection pulsed through her body as she yearned for him to hold her again. He opened a drawer, producing a taper candle and a lighter.

"Have you ever played with hot wax before."

"No, I haven't. Will it hurt?"

"That is the whole point. The pleasure from the pain..."

"Is there anything to put on first, to ease the aftermath?"

"Some people use petroleum jelly, but I think that is for amateurs. But, if you are really scared, I have something else that will calm your nerves." He produced a bong and some pot out of the same drawer. It seemed all his little secrets were hidden in there.

"OK. I'm down then."

He laughed at her. "Oh, you are so cute, my little southern belle," he said, as he moved closer to the bed. He lit the bong, took a few deep breaths, then handed it to her. She had only done this once before at a college party, but she thought she faked it well. That is until she coughed out all the smoke, leaving her throat burning as other parts of her surely would be soon.

Mark laughed at her again. "It looks like I will have to show you everything tonight, won't I?"

Miley laughed too. Maybe it was because the pot was starting to put her at ease, or from fatigue as the night was moving into early morning. It must be going on 5:00AM by now.

Miley and Mark took turns kissing each other's bodies and taking hits of the marijuana. Mark began to chew on her left nipple, harder now than he had in the car. She knew that the pot would dull her sensations, but it still reached the point where she had to cry out in pain.

"Oh, just the right time for this then," he said, grabbing the candle and lighting it. A faint vanilla smell mixed with the pot in the room. Miley wondered if he had stolen these candles from his mother's house. Maybe they had been set on the dining room table year after year in front of all the beloved family for Thanksgiving and Christmas. Now they were being used for foreplay. Miley laughed at the thought, which only led Mark to bust out a devious grin as he hung over her. She knew she should be scared, but she couldn't summon the emotion at the present time. The sexiest man she had ever been with had her naked on his bed. She wanted this. She always had.

He tilted the taper and the wax poured off onto her nipple. She screamed in pain. Mark began to thrum the hot bud between her legs. "This will help. This will make it feel all better," he murmured to her, then bent his head to bite her right nipple.

"Ah, stop," she moaned.

"Now, do you really want me to stop?" he asked.

"No," she whimpered.

This time, the wax hitting her raw nipple in conjunction with his fingers toiling against her sent her into a heightened orgasm that she didn't want to come down from. He moved the candle over her stomach, keeping it horizontal. Now, instead of one big rush, it dripped each drop onto her, searing her skin dark pink, seeming to be an eternity between each drop. The anticipation was driving her crazy.

"Mark," she breathed. He set the candle aside then, seizing her mouth in a completely captive kiss.

"Do you want more?" he breathed.

"Yes."

"Sorry. Now it is my turn," he teased her, lying down next to her on the bed.

"You want me to... hurt you?"

"Yes. Please. And be quick, because I need to take care of this raging hard-on soon."

Miley sat on top of him, straddling him. Unsure how to begin, Miley started as he had. She bit his nipples, then followed by pouring the wax onto them. Mark's body contorted under her, his face a complete mask of pained pleasure. She began to see how both sides of this could be fun. She bit at his neck, new inspirations coming to her. She tipped the candle to the sensitive skin on the side of his neck, using the hickey she had just given him as a target.

"Ah, shit! You little bitch," he screamed. "You will pay for that later," he intoned more calmly.

Miley simply giggled in response, feeling the weight of the wax still stuck to her tender nipples pulling gently against them. She dripped the wax down Mark's chest, watching it stick to the few dark hairs there, trying to run into the creases of his tight abs before cooling. She studied them constricting under the irritating heat. He bucked under her. She would need her own release again shortly. Her heat throbbed with her urgent need.

As Mark moved again, some wax dripped on his dick.

"Oh, that's it. You are going to get it now." He pushed her off of him.

Miley could only laugh as he took the candle from her, rolling her onto her stomach. He pinned her down and put the flame to her buttocks, letting it lick her skin.

"Ah! You asshole," she screamed and laughed, wishing he would just nail her already.

He touched the flame to her ass, again and again, until she begged him to stop. Then she felt his cock at her ready opening. He spanked her on the fresh burns at the same time that he plowed into her. She cried out, but could no longer even name the feeling. She lost herself in this sea of sensations as he thrust into her, over and over again. He seemed to only be out to satisfy himself now, but it was what she needed as well. Her mind escaped into the euphoria of lust. And when he ripped the wax off her nipple at the same time he came, all she could do was scream as he growled from behind her.

13

Miley rode back to the hotel in a cab the next day. Mark assured her he would have taken her himself, but he had an audition to get to. And she had no reason not to believe him. He had just taken a shower. With Miley. She had been a little startled to see in the light of day all the damage they had done to each other. Mark seemed unfazed. Miley had asked if all the bruises, bite marks, scratches, and burns would cause any complications for filming. He assured her that that is what makeup was for. He was only really concerned about keeping his face and hair unharmed. Miley saw her phone in her purse, but resisted the urge to turn it on. She knew it would be filled with messages from people worried sick about her. But Miley was still living in her own dream world.

Mark Tennyson was the handsomest guy she had ever seen. And now, after last night, she had seen all of him. She felt giddy! She felt like when she was fourteen and had a crush on the latest boy band. Except, this was so much better than kissing a poster until all the colored ink printed over the lips wore off. This was THE REAL THING!

Miley climbed out of the cab, giving a little wave to the driver, but he didn't care. He had already been prepaid by Mark when he had picked her up. Miley knew she should be doing a walk of shame up to her room at noon on Sunday in her club clothes, but she just couldn't help herself. She was smiling like an idiot. Laughing! There might as well have been cartoon birds flying over her head like in a ridiculous animated classic. Miley felt like this the whole way through the lobby and up on the elevator.

Except one of those birds was named Kiley, and it was about to crap all over her happiness the instant she swiped her keycard and pushed open that door.

"OH MY GOD! WHERE IN THE HELL HAVE YOU BEEN?"

"Um, where I told you I was going. To a club," Miley offered a kernel of truth, or something in the neighborhood of it.

"Ah, but you forgot that while I saw through your devious plan, you never actually SAID you were going to a club. And you never said WHICH club."

"Well, you knew I wanted to go."

"So WHERE have you been for the last seventeen hours?"

"I am an adult, and I don't have to tell you anything. And if I did, you wouldn't believe me."

"Fine, whatever! I hope you get treated for whatever diseases you caught last night."

"Oh, I don't think Mark Tennyson has any diseases."

"You are so naïve. It doesn't matter what someone's name is, anyone can— Wait, what? Mark TENNYSON."

Ha, Miley thought. Mark was so famous, even out-of-it Kiley knew who he was.

"Oh ya. I met him at the Blue Diamond. He took me to the Hollywood sign at night... Then his house." Miley saw the shock and admiration pass across her sister's face. But just as quickly it was replaced with a look of disapproval. Miley could actually see the gears shifting in her sister's brain. Kiley was judging her on her choices, as she had since they were in high school.

"Are you going to see him again?" Kiley asked. She always knew how to boil a situation down to the one definitive question or statement. Maybe that was what made her a good writer. If Miley could figure out her formula, maybe she could become a famous author as well. Miley wondered why she hadn't absorbed any of that talent while in the womb with her. Not that she cared about the written word necessarily, but having fans would be lovely. She realized Kiley was still waiting for her response.

"Yes. In fact, he is going to come pick me up for dinner."

"Why didn't you just stay at his place?" Kiley accused.

"Well, Miss Twenty Questions, he had an audition to get to." Miley went into the bathroom to take off her binding dress and put on her pajamas.

"I hope he looks better than you do then or he will never get the part," Kiley shouted through the door.

"I'm just tired! We had a—um, busy night."

"You look like a hard-partying zombie."

"Zombies are hot right now. Maybe he is auditioning for a zombie movie," Miley conjectured.

"Watch yourself, OK?"

"You make it sound like he is in the mob or something," Miley said, coming out of the bathroom.

"He COULD be," she said.

Kiley's phone rang.

"It's for you." She handed the phone to Miley without even checking the caller ID. But Miley did.

"Jane? You told Jane!"

"You didn't come home or call or even have your phone on. I was losing my mind sitting here worried about you," Kiley said.

"So you called an even BIGGER worrier to dream up even worse scenarios!"

"You better hurry up and answer it before she thinks the Mexican drug lords have kidnapped me too."

Miley let out a very loud, annoyed sigh, then hit the green button on Kiley's phone.

"It's Miley. I am fine. Stop having a cow. Just shove it back in where it came from," Miley declared abruptly.

"MILEY! I was SO WORRIED ABOUT YOU! Where were you?" Jane thundered through the phone.

"Um." Miley had not hesitated to brag and tell mostly the truth to Kiley. But Jane was more fragile. Jane wouldn't take Miley's being plowed by a movie star she barely knew all night quite as lightly. This had to be handled delicately.

"I went out by myself. I met a movie star. He wanted to show me around town. We just lost track of time."

"Why didn't you have your phone on?" Damn. Another good question. "To spite Travis" was probably not an acceptable reason for Jane.

"I didn't realize it was off. That is how wrapped up in each other we were."

Kiley slapped Miley hard on the back, making a retching sound.

"Who was this guy?"

"Mark Tennyson."

"Wow. Um, he is very hot," Jane replied.

"He is even hotter... in person." Miley added the pause mostly to elicit a reaction out of Kiley. It worked. Kiley hit her again.

"That is nice for you, but you have to realize you can't go out in a strange city all by yourself leaving us all sick with worry about where you are."

"Yes, Jane. I'm sorry. It won't happen again. Kiley won't overreact and call you again." Miley received another hit from Kiley, which she returned. "From now on, Kiley will know where I am when I am not in the room. I'll be with Mark."

"Last night, you didn't…," Jane trailed off.

"No, no. But he is a great guy."

"Do I have to call you every night at curfew or can I trust you to not become a missing person again?"

"I'll be good." Miley crossed her fingers behind her back as she said this. Kiley grabbed her fingers and bent them backwards.

"OW!" Miley cried out loudly into the phone.

"What's wrong?" Jane asked.

"Sister abuse. I gotta go."

"Yes. I have to go too. Ethan is crying again. He's been sick. I think it's an ear infection."

"Talk to ya later."

"Bye," Jane said, sounding very far away and helpless back in Alabama.

Miley threw herself back on the bed. She was so exhausted, but in a good way. She felt like she had run a marathon and pushed all her muscles to the limit. The second part was true.

"Do you really think Jane believed that I didn't sleep with Mark last night?" Miley asked.

"No way. That is the girl who did it with Wade, the hottest guy in town, on their first date in the pond behind the bar," she said, lying down on her own bed.

"Sometimes I think that is the only spontaneous thing Jane ever did in her life," Miley replied.

They laid there in silence for a few minutes. Miley was beginning to doze when Kiley spoke again.

"Now that everyone knows you are safe and sound, you might as well turn your phone back on so Mr. Hottie can call you."

"Oh, right." Miley rolled over and picked up her cell off the overloaded nightstand where she had thrown it when she came in the door. She pressed the power button. Miley decided it probably needed a charge as well, and rummaged around next to it for the power cord. The little bedside table was overflowing with granola bar wrappers, makeup bottles, and shopping bags. When the screen cleared, a million voicemails and texts began to appear. Miley could watch the number next to the icons grow by three messages a second. But before the phone could finish cycling through all that, it rang.

"Crap. One more person," Miley grumbled. She felt the most guilt over this one because it should have been the first person she called to report the night's events and to check in.

She pushed the talk button, raised it to her ear, and never got a chance to say a word.

"Miley Fuckin' Riley! Where the fuck have you been? I don't even care where you have been! You have been unreachable for twenty-four hours. Twenty-four entire hours. YOU CANNOT DO THAT TO ME! Don't you understand I CARE about you? Don't you understand you are more precious than anything else in my life? Than my own life? Miley, God," Travis paused to take a deep breath before yelling again. She took the opportunity to say something.

"I know. I suck. It was stupid and childish and it won't happen again. But you have to calm down. You don't even know what you are saying—"

Travis began again, cutting Miley off. "You do know better! You do suck! You are stupid and childish! And I do know what I am saying. Miley, sometimes you are not a very likeable person."

"How can you say that to me?"

"How can I not after what you did? Running off and disappearing all night, with your phone turned off too yet. You are a self-centered bitch."

Miley winced at his use of the b-word towards her. "You don't mean that. You are just angry."

"No, I do mean it. This is just the first time I had the balls to say it to you. You don't even care how other people perceive you. You just live in your own little world." Miley could picture him waving his hands over his head while he said it. "I don't know why I put up with you. I need to come to my senses and forget about you. I'm glad you are OK, but AHHH!" And then he hung up.

Travis had been seething with emotion. Anger, worry, something else? His words were getting way too serious. After all, they were just friends. For God's sake, she could feel his spittle flying through the phone at her.

She brought his name up on her phone, and then backed out again. No. She would let him calm down. She did feel truly bad for worrying him; for that long, anyway. Being on vacation, it was so easy to forget that back home there were obligations and responsibilities. She plugged her phone into the charger and laid back onto the pillow.

Miley replayed the first time she saw Mark at the club in her head. She thought about how it felt the first time he put his arm around her shoulders. And she drifted off to sleep.

Miley was awakened by the phone ringing. She lifted her head. A string of drool still connected her cheek to the pillow. She wiped her face with her hand, and tried to sit up. She looked around and wondered where Kiley was; most likely at the studio. Miley picked up her phone and shook her head to clear the sleep haze. It was an unknown number. But she had a good guess that it was the number she had not had time to program in this morning.

" 'Lo!" she said too excitedly.

"Hey. Ready for some more fun?"

"Sure!" Miley's heart leapt at the sound of his voice and her blood boiled through her veins double-time. He had called her! Last night wasn't a fluke! Mark really did like her!

Miley worked hard to hide it from Kiley, but she had had serious doubts about whether a movie star would really call her later—or at all. But it had happened! She could squash all her worries.

"I'll be there at seven. You said the Beverly Hilton, right?"

"Yes. I'll be waiting," Miley said. The phone went silent on the other end. Miley played the short phone call over and over again in her head. Her whole body vibrated as she pictured him last night at the club, in his car, at his house. A tremor shocked her body. Although every part of her was sore, she couldn't resist indulging herself before getting ready. She once again let herself think of his dark eyes, his hypnotizing smile. She thought of how it felt last night when he moved inside of her. Remembering how her body had reacted then, made it spasm now. Miley could not help but cry out as the pleasure spread through her.

14

Why was Miley kidding herself? She had thought her worries were over when Mark had phoned her. She would never stop worrying about being good enough as long as she was dating a celebrity. She had doubts while trying to pick out an outfit that would be spectacular enough for the occasion. She should have asked him at what type of restaurant they would be dining. She had finally settled on casual chic. She wore the skin-tight new black designer jeans that she had bought with all the strategic slices in them, letting her bronzed legs peek through. She layered a black bra under another new shirt, a sheer white number. Desperately looking around for the perfect jacket to finish the outfit, she had to admit that Kiley's black leather jacket with all the zippers she got for Christmas three years ago would be perfect. Trying it on only proved it. It had the right amount of worn that can't be bought at any store; it only came from natural wear.

While Miley waited nervously in the hotel lobby for Mark's car to pull up, she texted Kiley of her plans. Kiley texted back she had dinner plans of her own but "thanks for letting me know where you will be THIS TIME," making sure to use shouty capital letters. Miley began to worry when Mark was fifteen minutes late. She went out to make sure that the doorman knew what car she was waiting for, who would be driving it, and that she should be notified right away. The doorman looked at her skeptically, but nodded in acknowledgement.

At 7:30PM, Miley checked her call log to make sure that Mark had actually phoned her today, and that she had not hallucinated the whole thing. Then she checked to make sure her phone was on Pacific and not Central time.

At 7:45PM, his car pulled up.

Fashionably late. How could Miley have forgotten! She was used to good old, predictable, on-time Travis. Her heart constricted painfully at the thought of him. An image of his face came to the forefront in her busy brain. Other men wore a hard look, as if the act of maturing had been rough on them. Even Mark's impeccable appearance bore it. Travis's features were soft. His youth and innocence had yet to fade. Although his life had had its fair share of struggles, he was still filled with hope. It showed in the brightness in his eyes, the smile on lips, the glow of his skin. Thinking of him now and how angry he had been with her felt like a needle being stabbed into her heart, poison burning long after the image of his face in her mind had flickered and faded like film to a screen, having been replaced with Mark's. She cursed herself for bringing up negative memories of the past she could not fix at a moment that should have been holding exciting possibilities for the future.

As the doorman opened the hotel door to go in and retrieve her, Miley walked out. He opened the car door for her, taking the opportunity to peek inside. A shocked expression appeared on his face. Miley couldn't tell if it was a reaction to the fine car or the man driving it. As she slid onto the black leather seats, she saw that Mark was chuckling and smiling.

"What? Is it something I did?" Miley asked apprehensively, as the doorman shut the car door.

"I should bill that guy for my next car wash. He drooled all over it." Then he added, "I hope you weren't waiting long."

"Oh, no. Not at all." And he floored it toward whatever restaurant they were headed to.

Mark surprised her. She had expected some super-slick high-end restaurant for their dinner together. But he had chosen a trendy little diner that served only breakfast 24-7. Miley never would have guessed it from the exterior though. Looking in through the tinted windows, you could only see very dim lighting and black lights.

Miley was worried it would be like a Benny's, loud and gross and dirty. But it had the atmosphere of a restaurant that would have a more complex menu. They were seated in a round, black leather booth. The only color was the neon yellow, green, and blue accents in the stitching. They sat next to each other, but were angled so that they were facing each other as well. Miley was a little overwhelmed at first by all the choices on the menu: omelets, quiche, and specially-flavored organic sausage. Who knew breakfast could have so many choices? Miley ordered an egg and cheese breakfast sandwich. She chose an English muffin instead of a bagel. She asked for American cheese instead of Pepper Jack. She also added a slice of Canadian bacon on it as well. Mark ordered a fancy omelet.

When their order came, Miley dug into her sandwich and gave a little sigh.

"Ah, I see what you did there," Mark said, nodding and winking at her. "You just forced this place to violate patent laws and serve you an egg muffin sandwich."

"That I did," she replied, taking another bite.

"That's it. Next time we go out, I am going to take you straight to MacRonnell's."

"Mmm, I wouldn't be opposed to that. But I will only order off the breakfast menu," she said between bites, remembering how much she had stressed over what to wear on this date of mystery.

"How do you feel about going shopping tomorrow?" Mark asked, shoveling in more of his omelet. He motioned the waitress for more orange juice.

"That is what I was planning on doing tomorrow anyway," she said, trying to sound coy. She wasn't sure if it worked.

"I have to go get final alterations done on my tux tomorrow for the VTV Movie Awards on Tuesday. I was hoping you could come along to the store."

"That would be great."

"And if you are going with me to the awards, we should probably get you something nice as well."

"What did you just say?" Miley's head whipped up to look at him.

"Unless you don't want to go, I mean." He tried to play it cool. Sniffing in through his nose, he wiped his hand across his face to remove imaginary tears. He slid it behind Miley's back, pretending to look the other direction.

"Oh my God! I would love to!" Miley shouted, her fork clattering to her plate into the remainder of her hash browns, drawing the attention of the other patrons. She jumped up, bumping the table, and threw her arms around his neck.

"Ya, I thought you would like that," Mark mumbled in her ear. They then shared a long, inappropriately passionate kiss. They were interrupted by the loud throat clearing of the waitress.

"I would totally LOVE to be your date for the VTV Movie Awards," she told him, now half sitting on his lap. VTV had started as a channel that showed all music videos back in the day. That had birthed a music video awards show, which had then spawned a movie awards show as well. She watched it every year in front of her television with a big bowl of popcorn in her pajamas. When Kiley had told her the dates of the trip, Miley had assumed she would be watching it from their hotel room. While Miley believed in her ability to make her own dreams come true, she never could have imagined that she could materialize THIS.

"Wanna go back to my place and celebrate?"

"Totally."

"Ah, don't become a valley girl on me now. I don't want to have to kick you to the curb," Mark joked.

"Never," said Miley, kissing him again, even harder this time, if that was possible. "I must admit, just talking to you on the phone earlier got me all hot and bothered," Miley confessed to him.

"Oh now, you can't be starting things without me. You have to save that energy for me."

15

Miley couldn't believe she was waking up in Mark Tennyson's bed; to the sound of him taking a shower. She felt like a Make-a-Wish kid whose dream had come true; except with a lot more sex. Miley stretched her arms and legs out from her body.

"Ow-ah," she shouted out loud.

Fuck. What had they gotten up to last night?

Oh, the ecstasy.

Like, literally, the drug and the feeling.

Mark had introduced it. Said it would make the sex, the feeling, the connection, mind-blowing. And he had been right. But it also provided no common sense or regard for areas that may have been exposed to too much friction. Miley was glad she was on the pill. A condom would never hold up to all of Mark's rough sex.

"Hey, that's what you said last night," he said, coming out of the bathroom with a baby blue bath towel wrapped around his waist and nothing else. His hair was wet. This made it hang longer than it normally would down the sides of his face. His tanned chest, with only a small trail of black hair down the middle, still had droplets of water on it that glistened in the sunlight coming in through the curtains. Evidence of their late night encounter showed itself in bruises and abrasions across his well-defined muscles. He hadn't shaved his face since before they met at the Blue Diamond. The dark stubble that was taking over his chin made him look more mature and very sexy. But, oh, how Miley was getting stubble burn.

She was unsure what to do from here. A soothing hot shower for her sore muscles, definitely. But she hadn't packed an overnight bag. She supposed she could scavenge some basics like toothpaste and deodorant from Mark's bathroom.

"Can we swing by my hotel this morning, so I can grab some fresh clothes?"

"No."

"No?"

"Number one, because it is already 2:00PM. Number two, because we are buying you new clothes today," he reasoned.

"But what if I, like, want a toothbrush?"

"Oh, then just leave a list for the housekeeper. She will provide that for you."

"Wow. Staying at your house now ranks better than the hotel," Miley said, impressed.

"I try. C'mon. Get out of bed. We gotta get a move on. Unless, of course, there is a reason you are still in bed." Mark raised an eyebrow at her.

"Well..."

Miley let the hot water wash away all the sins of the previous evening, and the previous ten minutes. She couldn't stop smiling! She also couldn't stop picturing Mark in only that towel. Or Mark with no towel at all.

The things he wanted to do were dirty and depraved, but Miley couldn't help herself. She wanted to please him. And it seemed early enough in the relationship to set her own wants and needs aside if it meant she could stay with him longer. She wanted to be seen as eager and willing in his eyes. She enjoyed sharing the spotlight with him. If it meant she occasionally had to do things she didn't want to do in bed, well, that was just compromise, wasn't it? What every relationship was built on?

She remembered she would have to call Kiley while they were in the car. It was overdue time to check-in. She thought about calling Travis too, but then decided against it. She really wanted to share her happiness with someone less judgmental than Kiley, but she figured he might still be mad at her.

She decided it was time to stop using up all the hot water in California and get on with her day. After all, there was a drought going on. A whole day of shopping with just her and

Mark and his credit card? That was what Miley called a great day.

After they were done with Mark's fitting at the fine menswear store, Mark drove them to a side street in Beverly Hills, lined with clothing stores. Miley thought this must be what heaven looked like. Mark found a parking spot to slide his sports car into on the street. They each got out of the car and when he walked up next to her, he hung his arm around her shoulders in the familiar way he always did. Miley felt like she was floating along the sidewalk next to him. But she was quickly brought back down to earth when she saw June standing out in front of a nearby store.

"Late as usual, Mr. Tennyson. Hi Miley! Great to see you again," June gushed. Miley tried to assess if June was on any mood-altering substances. But not knowing her true personality made it difficult for Miley to judge.

"Hey, I am blaming all this tardiness on Miley. She couldn't manage to get out of bed," Mark chuckled.

"I bet," said June. She gave Miley a wink as the couple drew closer to where she was waiting on the sidewalk.

Miley blushed against her will. "What's June doing here?" she whispered to Mark barely out of June's earshot as they approached her.

"I invited June along to help you shop. I'm a guy. I won't really be of any help to you. Don't worry. She is an excellent shopper. She has spent much of my money in the past," Mark said, responding to Miley's question without making it sound like he was.

"Everything he says is true. Especially the part where he won't be of any use to you," June gushed.

Mark gave her the finger.

"C'mon," she yelled, grabbing Miley's hand and towing her along. They busted through the doors into the first store.

Miley had her doubts. June seemed to dress like a member of the granola set. But looking closer, Miley could tell her outfits were coming off the racks at expensive boutiques and not from the common man's thrift store on the corner. After a couple stores, Miley had to admit that it was a lot of fun shopping with another woman who was actually as enthusiastic about shopping as she was. Kiley could not be included in that category.

As the women tried on clothes and kept the saleswoman busy fetching different sizes, Mark sat around and watched. He talked on his phone and typed several emails. In his words, he had "some big things in the pipeline" that he was working on.

In one store, June made Miley try on a red cheongsam dress with little black flowers printed on it imported from China. It was form-fitting and short, stopping a few inches above Miley's knees. It was made with the finest silk. How fine? So fine the store didn't bother to put a price tag on it. But when she came out of the dressing room, Mark's eyes visibly widened.

"I think that's the dress," he said, getting up and approaching her.

"This? I like it, but for an awards show?" Miley said, looking down at herself in the dress again. Mark rotated her and wrapped his arms around her so that she could see her own reflection in the three-way mirror outside the fitting rooms.

"It is the VTV Movie Awards. It is not black tie. And look at those legs. Mmm." Mark leaned down and put his hand on Miley's ankle. He ran his hand all the way up her leg and up her dress. The saleswomen seemed to disappear at this point. It seemed like the kind of store that could only handle one customer at a time anyway.

"Maybe." Miley tried to keep her breathing normal. "It needs some black strappy high heels."

"No, no. Something flat," Mark said as he kissed the back of her neck and cupped her breasts in his hands.

"Really?" Miley said, her voice breaking.

"Really." Mark turned her toward him and they kissed. He put his hands on her ass and pushed her against him. She could feel how much he liked her in the dress. He backed her toward the dressing room, still kissing her. As they pushed through the door, he ran his hands up under the back of her dress, baring her ass except for her thong. He smiled as he studied it in the mirror behind her. No one had been in sight in the store. Even June had disappeared.

He rotated Miley around so that her back was to his front. He cupped her left breast, his hand on top of the silky material as he kissed her neck. With his other hand, he unfastened the fly of his jeans, shoving his pants down to expose his manhood. He was a movie star who wanted her constantly. There was no way she would say no to him. He smiled an evil grin at her in the mirror as he peeked over her shoulder. A hunk of his black hair fell over his forehead.

When they left that store, a flock of paparazzi had appeared outside. June and Mark acted disgusted to be bothered with the inconvenience, but never tried to hide their faces. Mark even talked to some of them. Very casual, of course. The rest of the day they were followed. The photographers stayed outside the stores on the sidewalk when they entered, waiting for them to reemerge. Miley could only guess some Hollywood business law prevented them from entering.

"You guys probably hate it, but for a newcomer it is fun to have my picture taken that much," Miley confided to June, glancing out the window as they surveyed more merchandise.

"Who do you think called all those photogs?" June said, raising an eyebrow so blond, it was almost invisible.

"I don't know. The sales ladies at the store?" Miley guessed.

"Did you see any of THEM on the phone while we were there?"

"No, but—" Then Miley got what June meant. Mark had called them himself.

"Really?" Miley asked, scrunching up her face in disbelief.

"It wouldn't be the first time," June said, adding a scarf to her purchase pile.

"Oh, I've still got to get shoes for the dress... I still think heels would look better," Miley mused.

"Oh, heels would totally look better. But then you would tower over your date. And that doesn't look so good in the magazines."

"That's why I can't wear heels?" Miley stated in wonder.

"Of course. I take it you haven't dated an actor before... Oh ya, that's right: Alabama. You know, we have spent all day together and I don't even notice your accent anymore."

Miley tried on some shoes and asked June to critique. They settled on a pair of black ones in a slipper-like style. At least her feet would be more comfortable than the starlets that were attending.

"June, can I ask you a question?" Miley began.

"Sure," she replied.

"What is the deal between you and Mark. Is it anything I should be worried about?"

"Oh, hell no. He is all eyes for you right now. Him and I, we didn't mesh. We are still friends with benefits, I suppose. And one of the benefits is occasional shopping trips," June said smiling, holding up a gold necklace. June didn't list the other benefits. "I suppose if I got a starring role in a movie he might want me to escort him to an awards show or two. But that isn't likely to happen anytime soon," she said, her tone at the end conveying disappointment.

"Well, that's good, I guess. I mean, that you and Mark don't have anything going on right now."

"Don't worry about it. I don't want you to feel threatened in any way. I actually have lots of fun hanging out with you. I hope we can do it again real soon," June said earnestly.

"Oh, me too. I've had a great time today," Miley said, and she meant it.

"Hey, did you guys get enough loot? Can we call it a night yet?" Mark came in and put his arm around Miley, glancing at the few items she was holding on to. "I like those shoes," he said.

"I bet you do," said June, exchanging a knowing glance with Miley.

16

Miley woke up with major jitters. She had never been on a red carpet in her life. There must be, like, pointers and secrets that she was going in blind about. At least Mark had professional makeup and hair people coming to prepare them. Mark's maid Carmelita steamed all the wrinkles out of Miley's dress. Miley worried how to hide the bruises on her wrists from the handcuffs the night before. She rubbed her left hand around her right wrist, trying to massage it to make the pulled muscles feel better. All she accomplished was to confirm that they were indeed still painful. Then she remembered all the bracelets June had urged her to buy, still resting in the shopping bag. Miley assured her over and over that she was not really a bracelet kind of girl, but June had insisted.

June knew a little TOO much. Miley shook her head, removing the thought.

Miley and Mark were prepped and ready to go hours before the awards show was slated to begin. Miley was afraid to move, as she didn't want to ruin her hair or makeup. The stylist had left her hair down and straightened it. She had given her a few bangs. Miley thought a nice updo would have been easier to ignore all night. Miley was not accustomed to using so much hair product when she wore it down, but the stylist assured her it would keep down frizz, and her hair would still move, even though Miley was skeptical.

The extra hours went quickly. There was driving to the pre-reception. There was attending the pre-reception before the pre-party. Then the pre-party. Then driving to the auditorium for the awards show itself. Then waiting for what seemed like an ungodly amount of time in the line of limousines for it to be their turn to get out of their vehicle and enter.

Miley had butterflies in her stomach. She was hoping she would not need to take a nervous pee as soon as she walked inside the building. She could picture herself now, awkwardly asking Reese Witherspoon where the bathroom was. Mark was mostly on the phone with his agent getting pointers on what to say, should he win. Miley realized she didn't even know what category he was nominated in. It was amazing how much actual time they had spent together and how little they truly knew about each other. This only made her anxiety grow.

Finally the limousine pulled up to the staging area. Miley could roughly make out the fans and camera flashes through the super-tinted windows. Mark kissed her and, in the last seconds before the door opened, said, "Smile, don't talk. Let me lead." Then the door opened.

It was like Armageddon. Mark stepped out. Miley's senses were overwhelmed. The heat of the day rushed into the air-conditioned backseat that had, until seconds ago, been cool as a refrigerator. Sweat beads popped out on her perfectly powdered forehead. The bright sun combined with the camera flashes. She could not comprehend anything outside of the car. It was like trying to look into an active volcano: the heat, the brightness, and the shouting. All the individual screams blended together into one thunderous roar. The smell of hot asphalt drifted in as well, mixing with an antifreeze odor from the long line of cars left running too long in the hot day. Miley felt like she was going to throw up all over her crazy expensive dress. She could taste the bile rising into her mouth. But she knew Mark would absolutely kill her if that happened. That would not be a story he would want spread all over the news:

Up and coming star's girlfriend's lunch comes up all over. Film at 11. And streaming anytime on MEtube.

She may have hid in the car forever. But Mark's hand popped into the opening. Miley knew she had to do this for him. And for herself. This was her childhood dream, after all. Miley wondered if everyone was this terrified to have their dream come true.

Miley placed her hand into Mark's and let him pull her from the car. At least she didn't have to worry about a wardrobe malfunction. She had fought with the stylist over that detail this morning. Miley told her she would rather have a panty line from a thong than a crotch shot on the OMGz website.

Mark let go of her hand to pull down his tuxedo jacket until it was smooth. Miley thought she might fall over until he put his arm around her back and began to push her slowly along. He smiled, looking like Prince Charming. His jet black hair was perfectly gelled. He had his teeth whitened this morning. His smile was so wide that his shiny, bleached teeth reached up to his perfectly-chiseled cheek bones. He gave a little wave here and there, to no one in particular. The fans went wild. Mark was wearing the jacket, but had forgone the rest of the tuxedo, instead pairing it with a gray T-shirt and blue jeans, both of which showed some slight wear.

Miley was usually secure in her appearance. She should have been confident in her look tonight, considering all the professional effort that had gone into it. But she was not. Miley was shaking like a leaf. How did Mark do this all the time and make it look so easy? He must be a better actor than Miley had thought. Her face felt weird. It pulled and ached. She hoped that meant she was smiling, because she really could not tell.

As reporters stopped Mark for interviews, she found that she was able to focus on small details. Like that this reporter's false eyelashes had come loose on the right outside corner of her eye. Miley looked down and saw that the red carpet had had tears that had been repaired over the years with thread that was a slightly different shade. Miley gazed up at Mark as he smiled and talked. She tried, but she could not concentrate on what he was saying. This whole experience felt like having to do public speaking in high school. Naked. The next reporter actually glanced at Miley. She stood next to and a step behind Mark, in a subservient role just as one would do with royalty. She nodded and tried to make sure she was smiling. At one point she backed into someone. When she looked, it was Will Smith. He actually apologized to her. And he was every bit as tall in real life as he seemed on the movie screen.

A few minutes later, Miley felt something touch her shoulder. She quickly spun around to see who she had bumped into this time. But she hadn't hit anyone. It was Bobby Patterson getting her attention. His guest for the awards was standing next to him: his mother. It was a perfect way for him to hide his relationship with Christy, without alienating her by bringing another female who could be viewed as competition.

"Hey, stranger. Fancy running into you here," Bobby said. He gave her a hug like they were old friends. This pulled Miley away from Mark's side, which he took notice of, but kept on with his interview that was already in progress. Bobby seemed to have interrupted his own interview to greet her.

"I see I wasn't good enough. You had to find a bigger star to pass the time with." As Bobby said the last four words, his eyebrows arched up and his voice got softer.

"How is the movie coming along?" Miley forced her voice to work. The words came out only a little squeaky.

"Great, great. So sad that you and Kiley will be leaving us on Friday."

"Excuse me, is this the author?" the impeccably-groomed male reporter asked. Obviously Bobby had been plugging the movie moments before.

"No. Actually, it is the author's twin sister," Bobby boasted, wrapping his arm around Miley.

"Close enough," the interviewer's voice boomed. He had a voice for radio. Many cameras flashed at Miley and Bobby. Miley looked at the interviewer again and realized it was Ryan Seacrest. Holy crap! Miley flushed with realization that she may be in over her head. She started to turn to look for Mark. The weird thing was, her body screamed at her not to. She had some sort of strange, millisecond vibe that it was safer to be in Bobby's arms than Mark's, but she turned for him anyway. Bobby read her body language as meaning he should remove his arm. Mark was already coming forward to claim her, placing his arm on her in the spot Bobby had just vacated.

"Tryin' to steal my girl?" Mark said not-so-playfully, then winked. He wore his big, bright smile the whole time, but Miley could tell it was fake. His eyebrows had a deep crease between them. His grip on her was so tight it was wrinkling her dress where Carmelita had spent so much time steaming it out. Miley knew she had stolen the spotlight away from Mark. She knew this was a cardinal sin in his mind. She would have to be extra careful to not draw any attention to herself for the rest of the night to make it up to him.

"Naw, man. I might try to steal your next film from you though," Bobby replied, giving him his wink right back.

"Huh-huh. Ya, right" was Mark's articulate reply. "I'll give you a wave from the stage tonight when I win for Best Interspecies Kiss," he continued.

"I'm glad you have worked your way up from aliens to humans," Bobby smiled.

With that, all four of them were ushered further down the red carpet, and closer to the theater doors. Miley eyed that door as if it were her salvation. She consciously knew that there were just as many cameras and chances for uncomfortable situations inside. But she couldn't help wanting the illusion of the safety of the walls, the ceiling, air-conditioning.

She let Mark tow her closer to the doors. She was in his hands now, a willing victim for whatever he had planned for her within the belly of the beast.

17

"I am sooo tired!" Miley shouted, although the only other person in the house was Mark right beside her in his bed.

"That is because it is 5:00AM and you haven't been to sleep yet," Mark chuckled.

"I don't want to go to sleep. Then this whole night will seem like a dream," Miley argued, kicking her legs up into the air, before letting them hit the bed with a soft thud. "This night was like my lifelong dream come true." Miley began to cry as she admitted this to him.

"You didn't enjoy yourself. You were nervous as hell. I could feel you shaking," Mark mocked her, wiping a tear off her face with his thumb.

"That is true. But it was also a dream come true and none of it would be possible without you." Miley kissed him.

"It was nothing. A day in my life."

They laid there quiet for a few minutes. Mark rolled over onto his stomach. Miley began to trace his tattoo on his back, over his right shoulder blade. It was a white pool ball with a wide blue stripe, with the number "10" on it.

"Why did you get this tattoo?" she asked.

"Because tattoos are cool," he replied.

"But, like, why this one?"

"Thought it would look good."

"I don't believe that."

"It is for my grandpa," Mark relented.

"I knew it. Why a pool ball? Did you guys play?"

"Well, I really wanted to get my family name 'TENNYSON' across the top of my back. But, if I were playing a character with a different name, that would be hard to explain in a movie. And I don't need any extra time in makeup. I have better things to do with my life. I got the '10' for 'Ten-nyson.' Plus, my grandpa and I would play pool in his basement."

"That is really sweet." She played with his hair, combing it with her fingers. "It is nice to hear you talk about your family. I was beginning to think you were hatched from an egg."

"Ha-ha. Very funny," he chortled half-heartedly.

"No, I mean it. You are quite mysterious. I can't wait to figure you out," she cooed, gazing adoringly at him.

"There really is no mystery... No one else has ever asked me about my tattoo before. No one has been as curious as you before," Mark said, turning to prop himself up with one elbow and looked into her eyes. He held her glare, then he coughed, as if something had gotten stuck in his throat. She placed her hand over his heart, surprised to find it still beating so quickly.

"I usually like to know something about a person when I spend every night at their house." Miley was trying to use more delicate terms than "sleep with." She wasn't used to spending this much time with someone and having the relationship still feel so casual. "Did you grow up out here? Where do your parents live?" she continued. These were not details about him normally published in the magazines or on St★rDirt.

"Whoa," he exclaimed, holding his hand up in front of him like a traffic cop. "I am beginning to feel like I am being grilled on a police procedural."

"See? That is what I mean by mysterious. This is very common information for two people to know about each other who have spent as much time together as we have." Miley was dying for him to give her any sign that this was getting more serious. She was practically living at his house. How hard was it to get the upgrade to girlfriend? She knew it was a greedy thought to have. Most women would kill for just one night with him. Miley got to wake up next to him in bed every morning. This morning, she would be falling asleep next to him. But staring into his immaculate face and dark as coal eyes, she couldn't help wanting a greater claim on him. And her precious time with him was quickly running out. There were only two days left before she was supposed to be boarding a plane back home. It would whisk her back to her old life that she was no longer sure she wanted anymore. She imagined what beautiful kids she and Mark would have. She pictured their imaginary children playing with Jane's son Ethan and Kiley's future kids on Christmas day back in Alabama.

"I grew up in Iowa. My parents still live there. Happy?" he asked her with a smile.

"Ah-ha! See, doesn't that feel good. Iowa, huh? So you grew up in a rural area like I did," Miley surmised quickly.

"Nope. A townhouse apartment in downtown Des Moines. You need to work on your stalker skills."

"Hey, I found you at the club, didn't I?"

"To be correct, I think June found you. And then from there, you found your way into my car," Mark said.

"Then your bed."

Mark rolled over on top of Miley and they began kissing again. His body language and reaction told her he was ready to go again. Miley pushed him off and rolled away.

"But I am so tired!" she full-on whined.

"You are right," Mark said, trying to calm his breathing.

"I am, but about what?" she asked, puzzled.

"We should know more about each other. Can I come to the movie set with you tomorrow to meet your sister?" Mark asked tentatively.

"Of course. Um, I'll have to call and see when they are shooting," she told him.

"Cool," he said.

"Cool," she replied.

She snuggled up next to him to finally go to sleep. Mark wanting to meet Kiley? That felt like a small victory.

18

Miley's cell began to ring, blaring her favorite pop song of the minute. She scanned the screen, excepting it to be a call from Kiley. Her heart beat tripled when Travis's face, framed by his shaggy blond hair, illuminated her display.

"TRAVIS! I am so glad you called me. I wanted to call you and apologize, but I wanted to give you time to cool off," Miley gushed into her phone.

"Ya, I can see that you spent ALL your time worrying about my mental well-being. Why am I seeing pictures of you on the Internet at the VTV Movie Awards with Mark Tennyson?"

"Um, ya. That just sort of happened," Miley said. She knew Travis could hear her shrug through the phone.

"And that's why you didn't come back to your hotel on Saturday night?"

"Correct."

"Oh, Miss Miley. I should have known you would go out to Hollywood and catch yourself some star tail," Travis said, exasperated.

"Well, that was sort of my plan. I just never thought I would score so well!"

"You are such a gold-digger. Makes it really hard to like you."

"Am not—much." Miley found it hard to devise a cohesive argument when presented with the truth by Travis. "Mark is so hot and dreamy and—"

"He looks like a Caucasian Taylor Lautner," Travis said.

"What?"

"You know? The werewolf guy from those movies made from those books."

"You think?" Miley asked, wrinkling her nose in wonder.

"Yes. When he smiles, he has that same look. Like he has too many pearly white teeth in his mouth."

"Oh, I can see that."

"So, was that like a one-time event or what?" he asked.

"I'm not sure," she replied.

"Are you at his house now?"

"No, at the hotel. I have been at his place most of the week. But today he had some work stuff to do."

"Oh, well. Doesn't seem that serious then." His voice instantly sounded lighter.

"Travis!"

"What?"

"How can you say that! I am in LOVE, complete with all the hearts with arrows through them and fat babies with white feather wings."

"And does he feel the same about you?" he asked, skeptically.

"He must. He invited me to the awards show with him," Miley said, still upbeat.

"But you are coming home on Friday..." Travis meant it as a statement, but it sounded more like a question.

"We haven't really discussed that yet. But he is going to meet Kiley tomorrow," Miley said excitedly.

"Wait. You are out there on vacation with your sister, and this dude hasn't even met her yet? What have you been doing all week?" Travis's voice had an edge to it that Miley hadn't heard before.

"Mark Tennyson," she answered sheepishly.

"Aaah!" His yell came through loudly, even as she could tell he had removed the phone from his face.

"What? What bug is up your butt now?"

"I want what is best for you, Mile. And this joker, he doesn't seem 'right' for you."

"And who is right for me, Travis? Sandy wasn't. Neither were all the other losers in Alabama that I dated. Am I supposed to be alone forever? Trav, I plan weddings FOR A LIVING. I am tired of watching everyone else be happy and in love. I want that. What, are you going to date me?"

"Uh-mph." Travis started to say something, then it was muffled.

Awkward silence. What Kiley had said earlier about Travis was still burning in the back of Miley's brain. Travis? Pffft. Travis was a friend, nothing more. Maybe it was Miley's time for some happiness, to fall in love.

"See, Trav. This is my chance. Just let me have my chance at love. Be happy for me," Miley pleaded.

"Yes. I see your side of it. Good luck. I gotta run. Client appointment. Maybe I'll see you again sometime, or not."

"Trav, don't be like that—"

"Gotta run. 'Bye."

And he was gone. Somehow this trip had caused a rift in their friendship. Miley had no clue why.

TRAVIS

Stupid girl. Stupid, beautiful, smart, romance-addicted lovesick girl.

Why couldn't she see that this dork would only hurt her, like all the rest had? He didn't know how, but he knew it would happen. And probably sooner rather than later.

But would it happen soon enough? Before her flight home on Friday? Probably not.

And Miley had an event to be at on Saturday. Would she blow that off for some douchebag movie star? Probably.

And why couldn't Miley simply open her eyes and realize she should be with him? They were great friends. So great that that was why he couldn't come clean to her on the phone about his true feelings for her. He couldn't risk losing her. If they were only friends, that was better than nothing at all. He couldn't stand to not have her in his life. He liked her drama. He liked being the voice of reason in her off-kilter life. He liked being the shoulder she cried on when all the other jerks screwed her over.

Was that a little sadistic? To let her suffer over and over when he could end her suffering? Should he just tell her? He asked himself that question over and over again. He contemplated it as he drifted off to sleep at night. His logic always answered that she had to approach him. It was the best way to not risk losing her. But what if he was going to lose her now through his silence? What if she never came back home?

No, he couldn't even ponder that option. He would have to put his faith in Kiley to bring her back home again. And maybe he would give Kiley a little call, just to be sure.

KILEY

"Hey, Honey. Sorry I haven't talked to you much. I've been on the set a lot."

"Aw, that's OK. I knew you would be busy when you went out there. I'm busy here too," Josh replied, sounding tinny through the speaker.

"How is everything going?" Kiley asked.

"Good. Well, I mean, we have the usual construction nightmares going on: contractors who don't show up or electricians misreading blueprints. Yesterday the secretary couldn't find the permits while the inspector was here. Those suckers are supposed to be posted in plain sight at all times. But, even with all that, we are still on schedule."

"My God. You are really doing it. You turned miles of farmland into a big-time resort."

"Well, still working on it. Did you doubt me?" Josh asked, his voice sounding like that of a small child needing his mother's acknowledgment.

"No. I just doubted that it could be done. By anyone. I couldn't see the land transformed in my head until it began," Kiley tried to clarify.

"Oh, I guess I get that. It wasn't a problem for me because I had been envisioning it for eight years now."

"You have always been a visionary."

"I envisioned your second book being a hit, and it is."

"And such a different plot than the first book," Kiley said.

"I wonder what could have influenced that." She could hear Josh's smile through the phone. He never failed to miss an opportunity to take credit for being the influence for the male lead in her second book. He had provided the physical traits of the male protagonist, as well as inspiration for much of the more steamy scenes as well.

"You sound down, babe. What's up?" Josh asked.

Apparently Kiley's melancholy traveled through the phone as well.

"It's Miley. I thought we would have all this great sister-bonding time. But instead she is spending all her time with that actor guy, Mark Tennyson."

"Oh, I saw him in *Monster Fighters: To Hell And Back*. He was good. He had a very 'every man' quality. Does he have that in person?" Josh asked.

"I haven't actually met him yet. Miley is just way too attached to him too quickly. She is spending every second with him. I am afraid it is going to end badly."

"Are you listening to yourself? Love, or lust, is about attachment."

"I know. But it isn't only me who is worried. Travis even called me. He is concerned that she might skip out on her flight home on Friday."

"We spent every second together at first. And everyone on the planet is lucky if they have just one relationship in their lives that doesn't end badly. And usually that one DOES, because somebody has to die first. Unless it is a car accident. Or a double homicide. Or a murder/suicide...," Josh's thoughts trailed off.

"You have been watching the true crime channel again, haven't you? And after I told you not to." Kiley stopped short of giving him the "tsk, tsk" she used to receive from her own mother.

"Maybe. But I had to find something to help me fall asleep in your absence."

"You can't fall asleep without my warm body next to you?" Kiley asked, with sweet surprise.

"Actually, it's what we do that makes your body and mine all warm that helps me go to sleep."

"Oh, well, I am missing that too."

"None of those actor guys have turned your head?"

"Nope. I can't wait to get home on Friday and run into your arms and feel your manly facial hair scratching against my face. The guys out here are too clean shaven."

"Uh, Kile, about that..."

"What? You are going stand me up?" Kiley mocked.

"Now you know I would never do that. But, uh, something came up. I won't be home when you get there. But it's cool, cuz I asked Donna and she promised me that she would welcome you with a home-cooked dinner."

"Fine. I guess. I just miss you so much!" she shouted into the phone.

"Aw, I miss you too, baby. I promise we will 'reconnect' when you get back. I will give you one of those back massages you like so well."

"Mmm. That does sound good."

"Then I will kiss you on that special spot on the nape of your neck that gives you shivers," he said, deepening his gravelly voice.

"You are going to have to stop now, or fly out here tonight."

"OK, I'll stop. I gotta stay here and supervise construction of my baby. I have to watch out for my investors' best interests."

"Hey, don't forget that I am one of those investors as well."

"Ah, your contribution was the biggest."

"No, it wasn't," Kiley argued.

"Not monetarily, but you can't argue that you have contributed a lot to the cause."

"Oh, well, yes. If you put it that way," she agreed.

"And Kiley?"

"Ya?"

"Don't let Miley bother you, OK? She is a big girl. Let her make her own mistakes."

"I know. You are right. But this mistake feels... so major."

"Then so be it. Goodnight, sweetie."

"G'night. Love you."

"Love you, too," Josh said. Then Kiley heard the phone go silent.

Miley was right about one thing. Kiley felt like Josh was much more than a boyfriend. They really felt like soulmates. They both had big things happening in their careers right now.

They had to pay special attention to not lose sight of their relationship.

Kiley couldn't wait to get home and run her fingers through Josh's unruly brown hair, to see his smile that after three years still found a way to scare her and thrill her at the same time.

If only Miley were here to discuss these thoughts with. But maybe that is part of why Miley was so gaga over Mark. Miley had had to listen to all of Kiley's relationship happiness all this time. Maybe Kiley should cut her a break. Maybe Mark wasn't as bad as Kiley had dreamed up in her head. She would find out soon enough. Miley was planning on bringing him by the set tomorrow.

God help us all.

19

MILEY

Thursday morning, Miley and Mark woke up at a semi-reasonable hour (if they were nine-to-fivers, they would have been late) and ate breakfast cooked by Carmelita. It was so delicious that Miley couldn't help but eat two large helpings. It made her miss Travis's cooking.

Miley regretted having eaten so much as Mark drove them to Plateau Studios. Her butterflies were angry at the lack of room in her stomach to fly around, what with all that food in there. She was nervous introducing Mark and Kiley. Kiley would have her bullshit detector turned up to high. And Miley realized she really didn't care what her sister's opinion of Mark was. She knew he was good and sweet and that he loved her, even if he hadn't said it in so many words. She had never needed her sister's approval for any guy in the past, and she didn't need to start now. This newfound self-reliance made the butterflies less angry, but they were definitely still present.

The security guards at the gate were very excited to talk to Mark. They saw celebrities every day, but they were still impressed by him. That just demonstrated what a big star he was, or soon would be. They wanted to know if he was starting to film a movie for Plateau. He told them no, that he was only visiting. Both guards seemed very disappointed by this. Although Miley guessed it was against procedure, both men asked for autographs. Mark obliged them, smiling his gleaming white smile the whole time.

"Do you ever get tired of that?" Miley asked, as he pulled away from the booth and headed for Parking Lot C.

"No, not when someone is a true fan. I hate the people who just take it and sell it on online. Those guys are getting trickier and harder to spot," Mark told her.

"Do you ever want to go out and have no one recognize you?"

"Sure. But I can pretty much throw on a baseball hat and sunglasses and no one would recognize me. It gets trickier if the paparazzi are camping outside my house."

"What do you do then?"

"I go to my buddy Kevin's apartment and switch cars. I have a boring gray sedan I keep there for just such occasions. I leave my house as myself, go to his house, slip on my disguise, and tear out of his parking lot in my non-sports car."

"Wow. That is like some seriously sneaky shit," Miley responded in awe.

"Ya, I know. If I put that on my resume, I wonder if I can get that CIA movie I'd like to star in."

"Maybe."

They parked. A page met them with a golf cart and taxied them to the soundstage. Today they were shooting scenes toward the end of the movie. It would be the scenes where Cinderella, er Monica, disavows her rich lifestyle with her parents and stepsister to be with her prince in love, Dave. The stage was filled with a set made to look like the interior of a very expensive house. Miley caught herself wishing she could live there, even though it only had three walls, no ceiling, and a bunch of digital cameras aimed at it. But the furniture was so fine—vintage 1700s couches and Old English wooden hand-crafted tables. It made her sick to think that these items were merely parked in a prop warehouse the rest of the time, collecting dust. Miley had expensive tastes, but her own apartment was filled with furniture from Ikea.

Miley led Mark around until they found Kiley, talking to the line producer and the production manager about what she envisioned in her head for this scene as she was writing it. Kiley described it so well that Miley could see the movie playing inside her own head before any images were shot.

Kiley described how the windows had to be open and the sun pouring in. The curtains had to sway in the breeze. This was to help symbolize the freedom and happiness and light that lay waiting for Monica just beyond the walls of her house, which had begun to feel like a prison to her. The production team was arguing that it would save time and money to shoot the scene with standard conditions, which sounded like they amounted to closed curtains with a light behind them. Then they wouldn't have to bring in special sun simulation lighting or fans or have a semi-realistic back drop beyond the window. But it was the director's call on how to shoot it, and when Jack heard both arguments, it was no surprise to anyone that he sided with Kiley. The group then dispersed to go make the magic happen.

"Hi. Nice to see you, stranger," Kiley addressed her sister. "And I assume this is the famous Mark? I'm Kiley," she said, introducing herself like Miley wouldn't have done it. Miley dealt with people every day for a living. Kiley assuming she didn't have basic manners made this one of those few occasions where Miley wanted to rip her sister's head off.

"Yes. I'm Mark and I am famous. Nice to meet you."

Miley wanted to put her palm to her face at that moment. That was the absolute wrong first thing for him to have said to her sister.

"I've had a few people wait in line to meet me too. I still put my pants on one leg at a time," Kiley retorted back.

"Oh, I put mine on both legs at the same time. But my maid helps," Mark said, with a devilish smile.

Miley cracked up in spite of herself. Kiley shot her an unamused glance.

"I'm glad I get to finally meet the person my sister has been spending every waking hour of the last week with."

"So you've been looking forward to meeting me."

"Not really. I only wanted to see what kind of element Miley has fallen in with who makes her miss half her vacation with family," Kiley said.

So he was going to play the fame card and Kiley was going to play the family card. This could be a long day; or a very short one.

"Miley could have gone back to the hotel at any time. I didn't have her tied up or anything. Well, not much." Mark smiled.

Kiley rolled her eyes. Miley felt like she was in the middle of a tug-of-war fight, being pulled from both sides. Why was life always so difficult? Miley had never been this hard on Josh. Well, not past the first few months anyway.

"So, how is the movie coming along?" Miley tried a new approach. The only subject they could both relate to, other than Miley.

"We were back on track, until the studio moved up our release date to Thanksgiving weekend. That is both good and bad. But you would know that if you had been here this week. Or watched TV or picked up a magazine," Kiley preached.

"OK, I get it. I fell off the map. Can we forget about that and move on? Why is that good and bad?" Miley asked.

"Good, because now that the executives have seen a taste of it, they think it will perform better than their original projections. So, they moved it up to a very popular release weekend. A weekend that the target audience will have four whole days off of school to go and see it multiple times. But now it will be that much bigger of a deal if the audience doesn't show up," Kiley explained.

"Still, that is great to have a movie coming out on Thanksgiving weekend. I never have," Mark said, finally letting Kiley have a win. He was letting his soft side peek through some of the emotional walls he had built around his true self as a result of being a celebrity.

"But now all the post-production effects will have to be rushed. And there is very limited time for reshoots," Jack said, coming up behind them. He put one arm around each sister. "Nice to see you again, Miley. And I see you brought a friend."

"This is Mark Tennyson. He came to meet Kiley," Miley boasted.

"Nice to meet you, Mark. I've heard a lot of great things about you," Jack said, shaking his hand.

Miley wondered how a guy who seemed so nice all the time (if sometimes too stressed) could be an effective director. Travis employed the same laid-back management style in his business. Miley had found in her own experience managing others that some people only responded to ball-busting. Maybe people resisted her instruction because she was a woman.

"I've heard a lot of great things about you, too. I also came to see how you were tackling this movie. Must be hard to adapt someone else's vision to the screen. And to create it in a voice for a young adult/mostly female audience must have its own challenges," Mark said to Jack, suddenly becoming a charming boy-next-door type. It was like he was meeting a girlfriend's father for the first time.

"I'm pretty adaptable from project to project. And I don't know how the actors feel about it, but as a director I find it easier if someone draws me an exact picture of what the end result should look like."

"Young adult happens to be one of the fastest-growing book genres right now. And movies for this audience are growing in popularity as well," Kiley added.

"But I heard the next movie you are directing is a spy thriller. Won't it be nice to make a movie with more action?" Mark continued, as if Kiley had not spoken at all.

"Oh, that's all rumor. I haven't signed on to any new projects yet. I like to finish one thing before I start another," Jack said, dismissively.

"Well, that might be the official word, but the talk all over town is that you will be directing the new Loren Fossil script," Mark pushed.

"It's all just talk. If you'll excuse me, I need to get back to THIS movie. It was really nice to meet you though," Jack said, politely excusing himself.

"I hope I get to speak with you again soon," Mark said, with more energy in his voice than usual.

Jack nodded as he left them.

"Hey Miley, I'm gonna grab some grub from craft services. You want anything?" Mark asked.

"No, I'm good," Miley replied.

"How about you?" he asked Kiley.

Kiley shook her head in response. Mark departed for the table.

"Somebody is trying to get himself an audition," Kiley said.

"What? No. This is his business. He is simply interested in the movie," Miley argued.

"He is interested in the director."

"So what? He is always looking for his next project," Miley fibbed. She had no idea what approach Mark took in getting roles.

"Just be careful is all I am saying."

"Be careful? You make it sound like he is dangerous."

"He could be using you," Kiley added.

"For what? I am a party planner from Alabama. Do you think he wants to steal my traffic flow tips? Guess what. He can have them," Miley quipped.

"I am also worried about you physically."

"What?"

"You have that choker on, but it totally doesn't hide that fat red mark on your neck. I don't know what kind of kinky shit you two are up to, but you better be careful."

"Ya. You said that already. Twice," Miley replied snarkily.

"Oh, I wanted to tell you. Jane called last night. Ethan has been really sick. Everyone thought it was an ear infection, even the pediatrician and the emergency room. But then when they looked closer, it was really a urinary tract infection. They sent him to a specialist that did all these tests and ultrasounds, and it was all caused by the strangest thing..."

As Kiley prattled on, Miley was watching Mark across the room, not listening to her sister at all. He looked especially handsome today. He had on low-rise gray jeans, with a silver wallet chain hanging from them on the side. They were snug and accentuated the curve of his ass. He had worn black boots on. They matched the black vest he wore over a gray T-shirt. Miley wondered if it was the same T-shirt from the awards show, or if he just had a whole closet full of gray T-shirts in his house. She hadn't peered into his closet on the home tour, but that didn't mean it wasn't stocked with them in the house somewhere. And was that the vest from his tux? Was he going to wear it one piece at a time?

Bobby approached Mark then, and they began talking. Miley was apprehensive. She watched from a distance for signs of unrest and male dominance posturing. Mark had reacted badly to Bobby on the red carpet. Miley had blamed it on their actor egos competing with one another. But the men seemed to be getting along easily now. Maybe Miley could blame the exchange at the awards on her impeding on Mark's spotlight after all.

Bobby was taller than Mark; maybe by a good nine inches. In his wardrobe and makeup, Bobby looked younger. He wore baggy clothes a high schooler would wear. In actuality, they were very close in age.

Mark turned and headed back slowly, not looking as jubilant as he had before.

After Miley and Mark had only been there for an hour, shooting stopped for lunch.

"Hi Miley!" June bounced up to Miley's side and gave her a half hug. "This must be your twin the author. Righteous jacket," she added, complementing the black leather jacket with all the zippers Miley had "borrowed" from Kiley a few days ago and had not yet returned.

"Hi. I'm Kiley."

"June. Nice to meet you."

"How do you know Miley?" Somehow Miley was being discussed without being a part of the conversation again. How did that keep happening to her today?

"Oh, I'm friends with Mark. I was at the club the night they hooked up. I was actually the one who introduced them," June said, her smile so big she was glowing and possibly even vibrating like a hummingbird or a tuning fork. She always gave off a strange tree-hugger vibe, but it seemed stronger today.

"Well then I owe you a thank you," Kiley replied sarcastically.

"Oh. Someone doesn't sound happy," June replied in a baby voice. Kiley smiled in spite of herself. No one seemed to be able to resist June's blond pixie charms.

"I don't happen to think that he is good for her."

"Oh, no one is arguing that point. He totally isn't." June took Miley's face between her hands and squeezed it like a little old lady at a church would do to a chubby child. "But look at how happy she is," June said, pushing her lips out like a duck as she said it.

"Yes. I will give you that," Kiley said.

"I thought we were all going out to lunch or something. Tennyson said he was buying."

Mark came up from behind them then, putting his arm around the top of Miley's shoulders as he always did.

"C'mon. You invited me for lunch dude, let's go!" June barked.

"Kiley, June." Mark waved one hand in front of him, signaling for them to go first. Miley knew she should be worried about what June had said about Mark, but she wasn't. She just could not make herself feel any apprehension about this handsome man at her side. She looked up at him now and he gazed back at her. His perfect lips, his perfect smile, perfect teeth, perfect eyes. Her heart fluttered. "I love you! I love you! I love you!" she screamed inside her own head. She really had not felt this level of lust and obsession over a boy, uh—make that a man—since she had been in high school.

Yesterday she had caught herself writing out "Mrs. Miley Tennyson" merely to see how it looked. She had to quickly tear up the paper so that no evidence of her girlish silliness remained for anyone to find, including Carmelita. Carmelita still hadn't seemed to accept Miley as a part of Mark's household. She was nice enough to Miley, got her anything she asked for, but she still kept her distance. Miley wondered if Carmelita would do double-duty as a maid and a nanny, when the time came.

God, how silly of Miley.

Of course they could afford a separate nanny!

They had a great lunch at a local place close to the studio. They all had great big bacon cheeseburgers, except for June, who said she was dieting for a role and ordered only a plate of French fries. As the grease glistened off of them in a thick sheen, she only ate a couple. Ironically, she is the one who had seemed most eager to go out to eat.

There was lots of conversation at the table. It seemed they were all getting on famously, to use a Hollywood metaphor. But if you looked closely, June was doing all the talking, and everyone was purely responding to her. No one else was really talking to anyone otherwise.

The table got very quiet when June excused herself to go to the bathroom. Miley wondered if she went to take more drugs or regurgitate the two fries she had eaten. Probably both.

20

Mark laid down his plastic, paying for the bill for lunch for all of them. They stood, making their way to the front door, where one paparazzo lazily snapped a few pictures of Mark and his lunchmates. They rode back to the studio in the rental car that Kiley drove, as Mark's two seater could not fit them all.

Once they exited the car, June pulled Miley aside.

"Look, I have to take off. I have other things to do today," she began covertly, shifting her weight from one leather sandal-clad foot to the other. "I did want to wish you good luck with Mark. I know he isn't always the easiest to deal with, but I think it will be worth your while. I really hope that he begs you to stay."

"I don't really want to go back to Alabama," Miley agreed. June had known what was on Miley's heart without exchanging a word. Maybe June had the potential to be a great friend, not just a bird twittering through her life.

"I don't want you to leave any more than you do. I want you to stay out here and play with me longer!" she whined, bouncing up and down. "Push him, if you have to." With that, she hugged Miley and flitted away, off on some other drug-infused adventure.

Miley made a move to rejoin Mark, only to find him answering a call from his agent on his cell. He moved to the side, seeking privacy. Kiley walked up beside her to fill the space Mark had vacated.

"I wanted to tell you that I really enjoyed meeting June," she began.

"I'm glad. She has grown to be a good friend of mine. I was afraid you would be too critical of her. She has a bit of a drug habit," Miley allowed.

"Oh, I could totally tell that June is a drug addict. But she seems to have a good heart, despite that," Kiley continued.

"I do believe that she does."

They sat down and were quiet, watching the lights and cameras setting up for the next scene. Miley couldn't help but notice that her sister was in no hurry to sing Mark's praises. He walked back to them a few minutes later, a bounce in his step.

"Hey baby, you ready? I need to head out."

"Ya , sure," Miley agreed. "Bye Kiley." She tried to make as little eye contact with Kiley as she could manage as Mark put his arm around her shoulders to escort her out.

"So, I'll see you at the airport tomorrow. Our flight leaves at 10:00AM sharp."

" 'K, thanks" was Miley's only reply as she turned her back on her sister. There was no way Mark could have missed that reminder. And she knew he knew. He brought it up in bed a few days ago.

Miley wanted to approach him about it now; right this second. She wanted to scream at him until he begged her to stay. But she got into the car beside him and said nothing.

They ran a few errands, one of which was Mark getting his haircut for an upcoming audition. Miley didn't like his hair as well afterwards. It was short and had gel in it to make it a little spikey. In reality, it was probably only an inch or two shorter, but now Miley felt like she was spending time with a different person entirely. But she knew that it was all in her head.

They went back to Mark's house for dinner. He cooked food on the grill by the pool while they both had a beer. This should have relaxed Miley, but it did not. He made fish and assorted veggies. It looked good, but Miley had no appetite. She picked at her food and shoved it around the plate, but didn't eat any. Mark didn't seem to notice, so that was good.

After dinner they drank some more. Miley's body felt all warm and relaxed, but tomorrow's flight still nagged at her mind. They went for a skinny dip in the pool. That led to more. While they were in the act, Miley noticed Carmelita tidying up the living room before she left for the day. The living room overlooked the pool. Miley was so sad right now that she didn't even care who saw them in the sex act. Then they moved into the living room for another round.

When they were finished, they laid next to each other on the couch's large chaise lounge. Miley felt the well of emotion rising in her, but she could do nothing to stop it. She should be happy, laying here naked on his couch. But she only felt overwhelming sadness at the uncertainty of their relationship. She could think of nothing worse than leaving town tomorrow and never seeing or hearing from him again. This would all fade away into a hazy dream that would still make her smile, but she would no longer be able to remember why. So when the tears overflowed, she tried to hide them. She brushed them away with the back of her hand, then wiped the moisture onto the fabric of Mark's couch cushion. Hopefully it wasn't expensive. She may have gotten away with hiding the tears by themselves, but then a sob broke from her throat. That drew Mark's attention to her.

"What's wrong?"

"Nothing."

"I don't think it's nothing. Did the chlorine burn you?" Mark inquired.

"A little," Miley admitted.

"But not enough to cause all those tears," he surmised.

"No."

"What's up?" He sounded like he was talking to his friends on the basketball court.

"It's just that I'm going to miss all this when I have to leave tomorrow," she sputtered out, grabbing her towel off the floor to wipe her eyes and nose.

"Then don't go," Mark said casually.

"Really? You mean it?" Miley could feel her red eyes bulging bigger as her voice squawked out the words.

"Sure. Why not?"

"Oh Mark," she threw her arms around his neck and squeezed tightly.

"Sure. This is a great place to live," Mark said brightly. "Much better than Iowa. And I imagine more exciting than living in Alabama."

"Oh my God. I am so thrilled!" Miley exclaimed.

"And you already have a ton of friends out here. June, Bobby, Jack..."

"I'm going to start a whole new chapter of my life," Miley yelled, even though they were sitting right next to each other and were the only ones left in the house.

"But I thought your sister was the writer. Get it? A new CHAPTER?" Mark said smiling, showing all his teeth and featuring his dimples on his round cheeks.

They laughed and laughed together like two idiots at Mark's lame joke.

"Wanna celebrate?" Mark asked, when they both got their breath back.

"Yes," she told him.

"Are you up for anything?" Mark asked, his dark eyes suddenly hungry.

This was a terrible position he was putting Miley in. He had just invited her to stay in California. She truly did want to do anything to make him happy at that moment. But she also knew from experience that Mark could in fact put her in a terrible position. She followed the happy thoughts in her brain of Mark and his budding career, ignoring the ache swelling inside of her heart.

"Yes."

They both walked through the house naked. Miley couldn't help staring at Mark's perfect body as it moved in and out of the lights of the various rooms. The pecs on his chest shown as a result of minimal, yet consistent, workouts. His abdomen was toned, but not as hard as rock. The muscles of his back pulsed with his every step. His gluteus was squeezable to the maximus.

"C'mon," he told her, leading her into the bedroom. He walked around the room to the bedside table. A shiver of fear ran down Miley's spine. She had had various parts of her body abused by what had previously come out of that drawer.

He produced a small vile and a mirror. He placed the mirror on the bed, then shook some white powder from the vile on top of it.

"Nervous?" he asked, cocking up one eyebrow and smiling. His voice was especially deep and sexy.

"Yes," she answered honestly, something she seldom did in his presence.

"You won't be in a minute."

Miley gave him a skeptical look.

"Would it be less scary if you sniffed it off my ass?" Mark asked.

"Maybe," Miley giggled. He rolled over onto his stomach, turning bum-side up for her. It was so tight and plump. Miley just wanted to bite it. And she did, because she knew he would like that.

"Naughty girl!" he said. "No more stalling." He handed her the vial. She shook out a little row on his ass.

And Miley turned herself over completely to his desires.

21

Miley looked at her phone again to check the text from Kiley containing the location where she was waiting for her in the airport. Mark was walking next to her, wearing a blue denim jacket, dark sunglasses, and a baseball hat pulled down low over his forehead. Miley didn't think it was a very good disguise. He looked like either a serial killer waiting for the right moment to strike or a celebrity who had been awake all night.

They had gone to his friend's home for the secret car switch. Mark was very paranoid about the airport. He claimed it was one of the worst places to be followed by paparazzi, because there was no quick escape, such as a car or back door. The friend, Kevin, mentioned he would be having a big party soon. Mark indicated he and Miley would be there. Miley loved that they would be a couple now; that his life and her life were now intertwined out here in this magical land. So many things were simply illusions in Hollywood, but she and Mark were the real thing.

Now they slinked through the cavernous hub in search of Kiley. Miley knew it was very cruel to meet her sister at the airport, only to report that she was not in fact returning home with her. Miley also knew she should feel bad that she left the packing of all her things up to Kiley. But, for some reason, Miley didn't care right now. She was too happy. She had too much energy. Her sister would hate her for her decision to stay anyway. What difference would a few more irritations make?

They entered a waiting area with lots of seats before the "No Entry Beyond This Point Without Valid Ticket" signs appeared. Kiley jumped up to approach them. Mark collapsed into a chair. Maybe he just wanted to avoid the ensuing drama.

"Hi Kiley. Oh my God, thank you so much for packing up my stuff for me." Miley detected that her voice was higher than normal and her words were coming out too quickly. She could do nothing to stop those things.

Kiley very obviously looked between Miley and Mark, then back to Miley again. Miley glanced over to Mark, who was slumped in the uncomfortable-looking orange plastic chair, his head resting on his chest. Miley wondered how obvious it was that she had taken another line of coke this morning and Mark had not. There may even have been a faint snoring coming from him as his chest rose and fell at a steady pace. What was with the orange? Were these chairs leftover from the 1970s? Is that why they were relegated out here to where few people actually waited? Were they only here to take up empty floor space? Was having them here cheaper than storage? Cheaper than disposal?

"You are not coming back to Alabama with me, are you?" Kiley said solemnly.

This snapped Miley out of her ruminations on the plastic airport chairs. And she hadn't even begun to calculate the amount of germs on them after forty odd years.

"No! Oh my God, you are SO perceptive. Now, I still love all you guys: Mom, Jane, Ethan. But I have to stay, um, FOR ME. And my future. Please be happy for me," Miley rattled on.

"Are you happy with him?"

"You know how I used to have to make up fantasies with cute guys to fall asleep at night?"

"I thought you still did that."

"Mark is like one of those fantasies come true," Miley gushed.

"If this is what you want, I'm not going to stop you," Kiley said, not hiding her melancholy.

"Oh, Kile, thanks for making this easy on me. I thought you would totally flip out."

"I was here. I could see how this CITY," Kiley looked over at Mark, who now had some drool dripping from the left corner of his mouth, "has affected you."

"I'm gonna miss Alabama, but there are so many great things this place has to offer." Miley looked at Mark adoringly.

He scratched his balls briefly, then appeared to fall back to sleep again.

"I will call you with the date of Ethan's surgery. If you can't be there, at least you can give Jane a call."

"Ya. Right. Of course."

"There is one thing I am not going to do for you."

"Oh, don't worry. I can call and tell Mom."

"Not Mom. Travis," Kiley said.

"Oh. Ya. Um, OK. Ya."

"You have to call him. That boy is in—That boy worries about you."

"Ya, sure. I will."

"TODAY MILEY. Before he does something like show up at the airport or your apartment, and you are not there," Kiley scolded.

"Sure. Bye Kiley. Thank you so much for bringing me on this trip with you." She hugged Kiley like she was never going to see her again. Kiley's return hug had the same intensity.

"If things change, know you can always come home, OK? I will pay for your ticket. No one will be mad at you."

"One person will be." And they both knew who Miley meant.

Miley decided to call Travis before they left the airport. Better to get all the difficult situations over at once, and while she was still high. She was hoping her words for Travis would flow easier, and his would not have the same sting. His phone rang once before he answered.

"No phone calls while you are on the plane." Travis's voice sounded hollow as it echoed through the air seven states away.

"I am not on a plane," Miley replied, her voice now devoid of the crazy erraticness it had when she was talking face to face with her sister.

"Why the hell not?" he said in a cold monotone.

"Because I fell in love," she replied.

"And he asked you to stay?" he asked skeptically.

"Yes," she replied without hesitation.

"In those exact words?"

Miley skipped a beat in the conversation while she tried to remember exactly what Mark had said to make her stay. But the conversation was hazy in the wake of all the celebrating they had done afterwards.

"Sure."

"Miley, you can't blow your whole future on a Hollywood crush." He was pleading now. "What about your business?"

"Don't make this harder than it already is. Jenny ran the business by herself before, she can again." Miley heard sadness breaking into her voice, matching his.

"Have you asked yourself why it is hard? Maybe that is your conscience telling you to come home, that things out there are not as they seem."

"You aren't here. You can't understand. Kiley gets it. She was here. She met him. Talk to Kiley."

"GODDAMMIT! I don't want to talk to KILEY, I want to talk to MILEY! The halfway-sane one that used to live here up until two weeks ago!"

"I'm sorry, Travis."

"Well, that's—"

"I'm sorry you can't understand how I feel."

"That isn't an apology. That isn't how you are supposed to treat your best friend." He had to spit out the last word. "I would NEVER treat you like this. Don't forget whose shoulder you always cry on when things don't work out. Remember that this time, that shoulder is going to be two thousand miles away."

"This time it will work out," Miley whispered.

"I'm not convinced. And I am not convinced that you are convinced."

"I am," she said, trying to muster a strong statement with her two words, but it didn't work. The sadness in Travis's voice was draining all the happiness from her body.

"We could have been together forever, Miley." Travis was now crying. This was a rare occurrence.

"Now you sound like a stalker." Miley was crying too.

"I would happily stalk you until the end of time."

"You still can..."

"No. You are my obsession. If you are not coming home, then there is no point in keeping in touch," Travis said, pulling himself back together.

"No. We can still be friends…"

"No, I'm afraid we can't. With you out there in California, there is 'limited potential.' Phone calls are not the same as dinners and movies and couch snuggling together."

"But Trav—I need you in my life," she wept.

"Not the same way I need you in mine."

Miley had a feeling that they had stopped talking about friendship a long time ago, but she wasn't going to question that further. Not now. Not now that this was all ending. She sobbed. People in the airport were now looking her direction as they passed.

"Please, don't leave us like this," she pleaded.

"You are the one leaving us like this. Goodbye, Miley."

"No—"

Her phone screen lit up, signaling that the call had been ended.

22

After Miley woke Mark up, they went to the parking garage to the unassuming sedan. Mark let Miley drive it back to Kevin's house. It was an automatic, so she had no problem with the car. Being unfamiliar with the streets, Mark had to give her turn by turn instructions. He changed his clothes at Kevin's and seemed to now have the energy of someone who just drank twelve cups of coffee. They left, still driving the sedan.

"Aren't we going to take the sports car?"

"It is easier to use this one with all your luggage."

"I can't wait to get back to your place and unpack."

"Actually, we aren't headed to my place."

"What? Why?" Miley knew the shock and disappointment was painted across the canvas of her face.

"I told you I have an audition coming up. My agent just told me he got it scheduled for today."

"I could come with you..."

"Oh no, don't bother. Lots of sitting around and waiting. And you wouldn't be able to go in with me for the actual reading," Mark explained. "But I will totally drop you off at June's to hang out."

June was uber-excited to see Miley. Miley would have felt much more at ease had her belongings been safely tucked away at Mark's house. Instead, he had insisted Miley take her luggage with her in case she wanted to change. June made her go out for lunch and go shopping. As neither of them had Mark's credit card, it was only window shopping. June wanted Miley to agree to go with her to a carnival tonight, but Miley said she couldn't. She was waiting to hear from Mark. She checked her phone every five minutes for any messages. June started to growl at Miley whenever she caught her looking at her phone, but Miley ignored her and kept on.

At 5:00PM, Miley couldn't stand it anymore and called Mark. Her heart stopped as it rang. Her heart made up all those lost beats in the same second that he answered. He apologized to her, saying the audition had gone so well that they wanted him to go before the director, who was in Vancouver in pre-production. It seemed the film had lost its previous leading man, and they needed to cast someone ASAP so they could start learning the script. Mark had not had a chance to call her in his rush to get packed and to the airport. Miley was deeply disappointed by this news. This is not how she wanted to start off her new life in LA. But he reassured her he would be back in two days. It turned out it would be one day for the audition and another for a hair, clothing, and makeup screen test. He didn't say what the movie was, and Miley didn't ask. She was too sad. Now she had no choice but to go with June to the carnival.

"Isn't it a little early to be going out for the night?" Miley asked June at 6:00PM as they left her apartment.

"We are going to a CARNIVAL. Those things do close. They are not like Walmart that stays open all night."

"Was the Walmart reference because I am from the South?" Miley asked, sounding offended.

"No. It is because when I was a teenager in a suburb of Sacramento, we used to go to Walmart to hang out after concerts or the bar..."

"WHEN you were a teenager? Aren't you still?"

"Oh, no. I'm twenty. But I get told all the time by casting directors that I look too young to play high school roles. Go figure," June said, getting into her car, a beater with the hood a completely different color than the body.

"How were you getting into bars as a teenager?" Miley asked as she climbed in.

"My problems run long and deep. Speaking of which," June paused to dig a clear sandwich bag out of her purse. "C'mon. Join me in a lil' treat. It will make all the lights brighter and all the rides spin faster."

Miley held out her hand. Maybe this would make her forget Mark (and Mark's absence), at least for a few hours. And get Travis's words out of her head that were still nagging her as well.

23

"Voicemail received from 555-623-7720."

"Miley? It's Jenny. I thought you were coming home today. Was I wrong about that? I thought you were assisting with the Nirschl-Heiden wedding Saturday. I can do my best, but you still have a lot of the notes that are only in your binder. Call me as soon as you get this."

"Press 4 to replay, 7 to delete, 9 to save."

Miley woke up with a raging headache. Her mouth was so dry it felt like sand. Her tongue was literally stuck to the roof of her mouth. Pulling them apart felt like she had ripped off all the taste buds from her tongue. She felt a presence walk by and tried to reach her hand out to stop it. When that failed, she tried to open her mouth.

"Water" was the only word she could get out.

"I don't know what you are used to, but I'm not your damn maid. Get it yourself."

At the sound of the unfamiliar voice, Miley struggled to actually open her eyes. It was June's seldom-at-home roommate. She was as black as June was white. They could have been two crayons out of the Crayola box, with Miley as a "tan" somewhere in between. Although Miley felt like hell, it was a comfort to know that she had made it safely back to June's couch. She groaned and rolled over to face the back of the couch, wondering how she would ever be able to get her ibuprofen when she didn't know where Kiley had packed it.

She tried to retrace her steps from last night. She and June had run around and played all the games. Had they really played the games, or only grabbed the prizes? Miley wasn't sure. It seemed like they were moving so much faster than everyone else. They kept bumping into the other patrons. Those who had been bumped gave June and Miley dirty looks. But they gave all that stuff to children, right? Or had June used some of it to plug up the toilets in the bathroom?

They had eaten hot dogs and elephant ears and French fries until their stomachs were going to explode. Then they rode fast rides. Then they had stood behind the generators and thrown up. Apparently Miley was on the June diet now. No wonder she was so dehydrated.

She remembered she had no real reason to get out of bed until Monday, when Mark would be returning. But the pounding headache could not be ignored any longer. As Miley struggled to get to her feet, she saw the roommate heading out the door with a large red leather bag slung over her shoulder. Maybe the roommate had a real job to get to. She was mumbling to herself. Something to the effect of: "Damn June, bringing her junky friends home again..."

That must be what Miley looked like to her. Was the truth really that far off target? Miley had spent all last night running around a carnival being a menace. And the twelve hours before that she had been hopped up on cocaine.

Was everyone justified in worrying about her so much?

She was overreacting. A few ibuprofens, some water, some breakfast, and she would be as good as new. June chose that moment to bounce out of her bedroom.

"Hey Girlfriend! What are we going to do today?"

"Ugh. How can you be so perky?"

"Because I already took my morning meds. Want some?"

"No. I think I will just stick with breakfast this morning. Thanks," Miley said, waving her off.

"There is no food in this apartment, so we will have to go out. I know a great little Chinese place around the corner."

"Chinese? For breakfast? Anywhere around here happen to serve grits?"

"Oh, so you need a little taste of home? I think there is a pancake house on Wilshire. C'mon." June headed for the door.

"Can't I shower first?"

"I guess. But the sooner we get out the door, the sooner we can find some excitement."

June's habit allowed her to find excitement wherever she went. Miley simply wanted to curl up in a depressed ball in her pajamas until Mark came back. What she wanted to do most was call and talk to Travis and have it be like the good old days.

It looked like neither of those things would come to pass.

The next two days with June passed quicker than Miley had expected them to. June drug her, in a traveling sense, all around the city. They went to malls, parties, and even some tourist spots that Miley had not gotten to visit yet.

24

"Voicemail received from 555-623-7720."

"Miley? It's me. I need to know if you have made all the final arrangements for the Tanner-Seaver wedding on Saturday. If there are any last-minute touches, you need to either do them yourself or let me know. Call me please."

"Press 4 to replay, 7 to delete, 9 to save."

Miley was relieved when Mark called her on Monday and invited her out to dinner. He picked her up in his sleek black sports car. She hopped in the passenger side before the car was completely stopped. He leaned over to give her a simple kiss. She threw both arms around him and hugged him tightly. It was a bit awkward having to lean over the stick shift, but Miley was determined.

"Well, it looks like somebody missed me," Mark said when she released him.

"You have no idea. Did you get the part?" Miley asked.

"Oh, I still don't know yet. I want this part really bad. It could break my career wide open. It kind of makes me nervous."

"I know the feeling," Miley agreed.

"I don't really feel like dinner. Do you?"

"No," Miley said, liking where this conversation was going.

They went back to Mark's place and worked off some of their anxiety. Miley felt like she could melt being in his arms again. They ordered a pizza in the middle of the night. Mark ordered it with all healthy toppings. He said he had to be prepared to look his best if he got the role. It tasted like shit.

In the morning, he dropped Miley back off at June's. He said he had to meet with his agent and publicist. Miley told him she would be more than happy to go along. She was very interested in his career, and how all the pieces fit together to develop it. But he said it would be boring for her, that he would call her later.

She noticed that he said "call," not "pick up."

He called around midnight. He asked her if she wanted to go with him to Kevin's party on Wednesday night. Miley of course agreed to go. She did wonder why someone would have a big party on a Wednesday night. Mark told her that that mattered very little in LA. If someone knew where to look, they could find a party or social event every day of the week.

Miley fussed about what to wear the whole day of the party. She ended up borrowing something of June's, although they were very different body types. She borrowed one of June's colorful hippie dresses. As far as Miley knew, it was a casual atmosphere. Because Miley was taller and bustier than June, the dress accentuated her breasts and was quite short. June said the end result did not look like she had borrowed a dress from a petit, flat-chested albino, but that she was looking edgy (and a little slutty).

As Miley got in Mark's unassuming sedan, she felt like tonight was important, but she couldn't put her finger on why. She tried to commit every detail to memory, as if it might be the last time she would be able to.

The party was an odd mix of people. It seemed to be one step up from frat party on the party-o-logical scale. Kevin was an easy-going guy who seemed to get along with everyone. He was the type of guy to be a class clown in high school. He wore a baseball cap and laughed a lot. Kevin apparently had worked many jobs in a few short years: waiter, extra, lighting crew, construction, retail. And his acquaintances from all these different walks of life mingled together here happily in his small apartment.

There were empty cans of beer everywhere. There was also a keg in the corner, but maybe the line was too long for people to wait. Miley hung on Mark's arm as he talked with everyone in the room. They all asked how his audition in

Vancouver had gone, and they all reassured him that he would easily walk away with the part. This made him happier and happier as the evening went on. She hadn't even seen him take any of the drugs that were plentiful and being handed around all night. Miley would look at Mark, and he would look back at her adoringly. This was the attention she had craved. The butterflies in her stomach were all but forgotten.

Then Mark stopped in the kitchen to check his phone. Miley was people watching, and did not notice at first that anything had changed in her blissful world. Then she noticed Mark's knuckles turning white as he gripped the phone ever tighter. She glanced at the screen reflexively, knowing she really shouldn't be so intrusive. It was an entertainment news article about a hot young actor stepping in as a last-minute replacement for a new movie filming in Vancouver. Except, as she could tell by his reaction, the name contained within the story was not Mark's. He threw his phone across the room, and it shattered to pieces against the wall. A few girls looked at the wall where the phone had made contact, but no one really seemed to care.

"It will be all right," Miley said, then silently cursed her mother for automatically saying that all through her childhood. Miley had picked up the bad habit, even though she knew it was not always the proper thing to say in every situation; like now. Mark's eyes were all dark fire when he looked at her. His hand reached out and grabbed her bicep, pulling her closer to him as she tried to pull away. She felt herself cowering at his side, trying to shrink herself until he could not see her any longer, hoping it would cause him to release her.

"How will this be alright?"

"Um, there will be other parts?" she said, her voice shaking.

"I have not had a big break-through part yet," Mark hissed at her. "My shelf life gets shorter every goddamn day. You have NO IDEA how much pressure I am under. You come out here on vacation and think you have walked into your fantasy. But I assure you, the flip side is a nightmare.

"Come."

With his one word command, Mark pulled Miley out of the kitchen and down the hall. He opened one of the doors. There were three people in the bedroom. Miley didn't look long enough to see what they were doing. Mark ordered them out. Once they were alone and the door was closed, he spoke again.

"You are going to do whatever I want. You understand." It wasn't a question; it was an order.

Miley nodded her head. He flung her onto the bed. She should have been bothered by this, but all she could do was be thankful that he had let go of his painful grip on her arm. She realized what was coming next might not be pleasant for her. But she loved Mark. And this was the first time he had come close to actually opening up about his deep feelings to her. Once he had the floodgates open, maybe he had trouble finding a way to stop what spilled forth. She needed to find a way to comfort him. Apparently that would mean burning off some of his fury.

25

"Voicemail received from 555-623-7720."
"Miley?"

Why did Jenny always start a message by making her name a question?

"It's me again. I need to know if you will be here on Saturday. You know we have two events scheduled and I can't be in two places at once. I mean, I suppose I could have Travis supervise the wedding. But it REALLY isn't his job and he already has his hands full with the catering. Call me ASAP."

"Press 4 to replay, 7 to delete, 9 to save."

The next morning, Miley tried to call Mark, before remembering that his phone was now a pile of electronic garbage scattered on Kevin's kitchen floor. She was at June's. Miley couldn't even remember the excuse Mark had given for dropping her off there. Maybe he hadn't even provided one. She was concerned Mark might do something irrational. He had not been in the best state of mind last night. She couldn't help but worry that he might end up another Hollywood tragedy. But she pushed that thought from her mind again. June told her not to worry. She said that Mark could be moody; that this was not the first time she had seen him like this. To be an actor, you have to have strong emotions, she had said. Miley was not so sure.

Miley didn't hear from him all Thursday. That evening, she made June drive her over to his house. Carmelita said he had gone out to buy a new phone.

She didn't even let Miley past the front gate. They spoke only through the intercom speaker.

June suggested a pajama party. It sounded lame to Miley at first, but they really did have fun. They ate ice cream and painted their toenails and watched chick flick movies. Miley made June watch *Sweet Home Alabama*, one of Miley's favorite movies, and not solely because it had her home state in the title. Not much else was very Alabama about it, as it was actually filmed mostly in Georgia. June claimed she didn't like to watch anything with Reese Witherspoon in it because casting directors were always likening June to her. It was hard to be an actress just starting out with no formal training and being compared to an Oscar winner, because you happened to be both petite and blond.

They also watched two movies that June was in. The first was called *The Zombie Killer Who Loved 2 Much*. She was a victim of a sex-starved zombie. Her whole part consisted of screaming at the top of her lungs when he had sex with her, and then again when he ate her brains out.

The second movie was a formulaic high school romp with a pretty forgettable plot called *Smoke'm Up High*. It had gone nowhere at the box office. But June had twenty lines in it (although all but three had been left on the editing room floor), and she was visible in almost every scene in the background. She said it was the movie that paid for her half of the apartment they were currently sitting in. Miley quoted facts and stats on all the actors, without the aid of her phone or St★rDirt app. She added the links between them and June to her mental six degrees list. June was amazed at her knowledge. She called Miley "an entertainment trivia savant."

On Friday, Miley kept bombarding June with questions about whether Mark really liked her or not. June kept trying to shrug it off, saying she was friends with both of them (and had been friends with Mark longer) and that this line of questioning made her uncomfortable. A few truths did slip out though.

"Mark must care about me, right? I mean, he came to the set to meet my sister. That shows how much he cares for me."

"Poor, naïve Miley," June sang.

"Why do you say that?"

"He went to a 'movie set.' He is an 'actor.' There is only one reason an actor goes to a movie set. He was trying to get a job!" June wailed.

"He wanted a job on my sister's movie?" Miley asked.

"Maybe, or he could have wanted to work on some future movie with the director or a certain producer."

"Oh," Miley replied.

"It is all about networking in this industry. Well, probably in every industry."

"Yes, I suppose," Miley whispered.

"I'm sorry. I didn't mean to tell you anything that I didn't think you had already figured out for yourself," June said, patting her back.

"I know. I guess I was blinded by love. Do you think he will call me?"

"Maybe he lost your number. Did you try calling him today?" June hedged.

"Every hour," Miley replied. June made a face in response. "Is that too much?" Miley continued.

"Probably."

"But he is my boyfriend. I am worried about him!" Miley whined.

"Did he ever actually say that to you?"

"What?"

"Did he ever actually call you his girlfriend?" June asked.

"I think so... He must have at some point."

"How about when he asked you to stay in Cali?"

"Um."

"MILEY!"

"I can't really remember—," Miley squeaked.

"You can't remember what? Him calling you his girlfriend or asking you to stay?"

"Either. Both."

"Jesus, Miley. Maybe your family is right to be so worried about you. If it wasn't for me, you would be on the streets right now," June said.

"Mark wouldn't let that happen."

"I am not sure you even know Mark."

"We have spent weeks together! Of course I know him!"

"Miley, it has only been fourteen days since I introduced you in the club. Mark isn't always the nicest person. He isn't big on other people's feelings."

"Why did you introduce us then?" Miley asked, trying to keep tears out of her eyes and sadness out of her voice, and mostly succeeding.

"Because you were miserable! Your vacation was not going the way you had hoped. You wanted a star encounter, and I gave you one," June philosophized.

"And you could tell all that by just looking at me in the bathroom?" Miley was angry now.

"Oh, honey. You had a crazed look in your eyes, like a wild animal that wandered into an amusement park. I could even see that with my beer goggles on."

"But I thought my little blue dress made me fit in."

"Oh, it made you look hot. But your apprehension was showing. I don't even know how you ever got in the door of the club." June shook her head.

Miley raised her head and smiled sheepishly at her. "I bribed a paparazzo to take my picture," Miley admitted.

"Oh my God, Miley! That takes some huge balls! How did you know it would work?" June gushed in admiration.

"I didn't. But I figured it was my only shot at getting in."

"Wow. You go, girl. Maybe we should go out tonight and you could pull that same trick again."

"I'm not in the mood to meet more guys. I only want Mark."

And with that, Miley sat on the couch and stayed there for the rest of the night, hugging a pillow and moping.

26

"Voicemail received from 555-623-7720."
"Miley? Is your phone working?"
"Press 4 to replay, 7 to delete, 9 to save."

June got Miley out of the house to try and cheer her up. June wanted to go to the zoo or the water park. She wanted to ride go-karts or play mini-golf—all the activities she could never get Mark to do with her. Miley finally agreed to an early movie and a late lunch. She wanted to be home by evening in case Mark wanted to take her out. June stuck her finger down her throat to simulate puking. She then medicated herself, probably in protest that she didn't get her way. Or maybe so that she could pretend that the flood disaster movie they went to see was actually an adventure water park.

Miley was thankful that she was sucked into the movie magic on the screen. Movies were always her go-to escape. It helped her to stop thinking about Mark for two hours and five minutes. But strangely, thoughts of him were replaced in her brain with memories of Travis. She remembered the many great nights they had spent watching videos together, the closeness they shared. Miley kept going over their last phone conversation in her head, trying to figure out how it could have gone differently. Every time, though, she saw it ending the exact same way.

She had lost Travis. Now she may have lost Mark too. She was left with no one to rely on out here in a strange city, where her only friend was a sweet, but highly-unstable, girl who could barely take care of herself, let alone provide emotional support for Miley. She fought to push this realization aside. She sniffed deeply to stop her snot, hoping she could make the tears retreat as well.

They went to a little café on their way home from the movie. It had a nice menu and atmosphere, but Miley wasn't hungry. June never ate much. Coming here seemed like a silly decision, in retrospect.

Miley noticed some of the other customers staring in their direction. There was a guy with brown hair and glasses, who appeared to be eating with his girlfriend. He said something to her, and she turned to look at their table. Another table with two women looked their way, with a combination of curiosity and disgust.

Miley wondered if maybe they had recognized June from some of the parts on her limited resume. June didn't realize at first. She was bouncing up and down noticeably in her chair. Maybe that is what everyone was gawking at. But it seemed more like they were staring at Miley. She had been photographed with Mark a lot in the past couple weeks. They had even attended the awards show together. So it was very slightly possible that they were recognizing Miley for being Mark's girlfriend.

So many people began to look that June DID notice.

"Why is everyone staring at our table?" June asked.

"I have no idea."

"Is my thong showing?" June asked.

"Maybe you forgot to wear it..."

They looked around at all the prying eyes. For a minute, the faces of all the customers went out of focus, all except those eyes. It was like the opening sequence of *Scooby-Doo*, with all the disembodied eyes appearing from the blackness. Miley's skin got suddenly hot. She felt as if something was gravely wrong, but she didn't know what. It felt like there had been a national disaster that she had missed on the news. Maybe an earthquake had just flattened a school of innocent children in China.

Miley tried smiling back to the table with the man and the woman. The man's face lit up. When he looked back at his date, his expression instantly changed to shame.

Miley smiled at the table of women. Once of them looked disgusted. The other looked a bit jealous. Miley's face must have displayed the shock she was feeling, because June started to get up.

"I don't know what's going on, but I think we should go—," June started.

The effeminate waiter came along right then.

"Can we get our bill?" Miley asked expectantly.

"Oh, that has already been taken care of miss, by the man at table sixteen." He gestured to a table to their right, and a creepy looking old man waved.

"And the tip has been taken care of by that woman over there." Now he gestured to the back corner of the restaurant where a woman was leering in their direction.

"It's nice to have options. Have a nice day," he said suggestively, clearing the mostly untouched plates as he left.

"We have to get out of here now. Something is definitely NOT RIGHT," June urged.

Miley was more startled by June's sudden clarity of their surroundings than the strangers staring at her. She let June lead her out to the parking lot. They were safely in June's car with the doors locked when June took out her cell phone. Miley could only tell from the passenger seat that she was doing an Internet search. Miley didn't know what for.

A page of text with a picture came up on June's screen.

"OH MY GOD."

"I thought you were an atheist," Miley joked.

"I am," June replied. "But you might want to start praying."

Suddenly June's phone came alive with a video. Whatever it was, it was mostly dark. The sounds coming out of the speaker were distorted. They sounded like wild animals; wild animals mating. But why would June watch that on her phone? Why would that make June's eyes do that crazy bug out thing they had done in her horror-comedy movie *The Zombie Killer Who Loved 2 Much*.

Intelligible words finally emerged from the sex sounds. A very familiar voice in a slightly higher than normal register, signaling pleasure. "Oh, Miley" was a moan in a man's voice, clear as day.

Miley grabbed the phone away from her as June thrust it to her.

"What is this?" Miley asked.

"Sex tape" was June's two word reply.

"Why would Mark send you this?"

"He didn't."

"I don't understand."

"Miley, you and Mark are the newest stars of the Internet."

"How did you find this?" Miley asked. She was fairly certain those might be the last words that she would ever be able to manage to squeeze out of her vocal cords.

"I just searched 'Mark Tennyson.' Number one result." June's voice sounded to Miley's ears as if she were speaking into a metal drain pipe.

Miley did not know how long she sat there staring at June's phone in her hand, while not really seeing it. Eventually June removed it from her hands. Miley wasn't even aware if the video had ended or not.

27

It was probably several hours later when Miley could comprehend a small fraction of reality again. June had gotten them back to the apartment. Miley changed into her pajamas, as she didn't foresee ever going out the door of this apartment ever again. But the outside world found its way in anyway.

When June tried to turn on the TV, "The Tape," as it should from here on be called, seemed to be playing on every channel. Miley felt ashamed about the tape getting out. What would her mother and father think? But she felt worse for Mark. This could end his career. How had it gotten out? Why had he made it? When had he made it?

"I'll just stream something," June said apologetically, reaching for a different remote control.

Sometime later, her roommate Kate came home. When she walked in the door and saw Miley on the couch, a huge grin spread across her face. It blossomed into a full-out laugh. There was no doubt she had heard the news.

"Oh, the newest Hollywood star is still staying at MY house! I told everyone at work, but they didn't believe me...," she began.

"Kate, cut it out," June said.

"I knew you had a 'thing' going on with Mark Tennyson. I just didn't realize it was THAT kinky—"

"Shut up!" If June had been a dog, her hackles would have been up. Under different circumstances, this protective streak would have been really sweet. But Miley couldn't help but think she deserved every single thing that was headed her way now.

"And the things you did on that video!"

"She didn't know she was being recorded," June said.

"By looking at you, I would not think you would be that bendy. You must have been sore the next day," Kate continued addressing Miley, as if June was not there at all.

"Stop," June ordered.

"It must have HURT; the things he did to you."

Miley rushed across the room to hold June back from attacking Kate. Her eyes were blurred with tears, but June was still an easy target to catch. Kate must have been satisfied with the reaction, because she disappeared into her own bedroom.

"I deserve whatever comes now," Miley said to June, in an even voice, holding both her arms. This was Miley's first try at testing how it sounded out loud. It would work. Every bit as strong as "One day at a time," if slightly more negative.

"No, you don't! I hate Mark! How could he do this to you! Just to further his stupid career!" she screamed.

"Wait. How could this further his career?"

"C'mon, Miley. Don't be so dense. You know as much about how Hollywood works as we do."

"But, I still don't—"

"Almost all stars become more famous after a sex tape comes out, especially someone who is trying to be seen as a sex symbol by the public. He used to joke about it, but I never thought he would go through with it. But he was so mad after losing that part. It was one thing for him to have no respect for me, but you are different. I can't believe he hurt you like this! I am never talking to him again!" June ran into her bedroom, slamming the door.

So he had planned this all along? Miley had been nothing more than a pretty body to make a sex tape with. Even through Miley's own haze of anger and astonishment, she worried what pills June might be taking unsupervised on the other side of the door.

Mark's attention had made Miley believe she was special, better than everyone else. But maybe in the end she wasn't special. Maybe she was simply an average chick schlubbing through each day. Maybe the sun didn't shine brighter on her. Now, it even seemed as though it never would again.

If she were back home in Alabama right now, Travis would be there to console her. He would tell her she deserved better than Mark. Too bad he hadn't told her that before she got involved. But she had never given Travis the chance to. She had turned off her phone like a pouty child. She had a choice to make between two men, and it appeared she had chosen wrong. Travis would hear about this soon, if he hadn't already. She could hear him saying "I told you so" inside her head, as he had on many other occasions. But worse than that, she could feel the echo of his disappointment that she had allowed herself to end up in such a situation. It was very possible that she was not even deserving of his friendship anymore, even if he would still have her.

Miley's curiosity got the best of her now. She needed to know exactly what was on that tape. A laptop lay nearby. Without knowing or caring whose it was, Miley opened it and click on the Internet browser icon. She found many articles with the sex tape, most with only clips with less than a minute of video. But she needed to find the complete video. She had to know the full extent of her literal exposure. Finally she found one.

It was nearly two hours long; probably the full length of an SD card. On June's phone it had appeared dark. In reality, it was low lighting, but plenty to see what was going on. He had staged the whole thing. Miley could barely recognize the girl in the video as herself. And why was she agreeing to these lewd acts? In a clear shot of Miley's own face, she had her answer.

This was the night she was on ecstasy. It was only the second night they had been together.

Had he been planning this since the beginning? It had crossed her mind before, but now was the first time she truly believed it. Sure, she was high on ecstasy. But she had never known of the recording taking place. She never looked at the camera. Mark had clearly looked into the lens when he set it up. Already he had been quoted in articles as blaming the pool guy as having a beef against him, stealing his property and releasing it. June and Miley knew that was a lie. But it didn't really matter who released it. It was out there on the Internet, gateway to the world; possibly even the universe. There would never be any way to remove all evidence of it. It would live on in infamy.

Everyone now knew her name, her stoned face, every inch of her body. Especially the parts Mark aimed toward the camera to better show off his own manhood. Miley did things that night she had never done before—lots of things. But she believed it was a private moment shared between the two of them. She was in love with him. How could she have been so stupid? Now everyone would think she was a skanky ho who did those acts all the time. She did do them on a second date with a man she hardly knew, if at all. Maybe the public was right with their first impression of her.

28

TRAVIS

"You picked a great night to hit the bar with me. There are a lot of sexy babes here tonight." Austin kept pushing his shoulder-length, dark brown skater hair back from his face. He was wearing his T-shirt that was homemade cut into a tank top, with sleeve holes that went all the way down the sides of his torso to his hips, showing off his muscles for the female persuasion. Travis thought he looked ridiculous.

"I don't know why I even agreed to come out with you." Travis sat slumped over the table in his usual too big T-shirt and denim shorts, his blond hair acting as a curtain, blocking his peripheral vision from the activity around them. It was already late, and he was dead tired from doing his job and Miley's both at the wedding this afternoon. It seemed the only thing worse than being abandoned by the girl you loved was having to pick up her slack. He picked at the label on his beer bottle. He couldn't manage to look around and even figure out if he had ever let Austin drag him to this particular bar before or not.

"Dude, this could be a big night for you! Step back out into the world again, Trav. Taste what life has to offer. Rrrrr." Austin always made growling noises when he saw an especially attractive girl. Which she wasn't, because she wasn't Miley. He continued. "You aren't still hung up on Miley, are you? C'mon! For Christ sake! She dumped you for a fuckin' movie star. Wake up. She ain't fuckin' comin' back."

"It's not that easy. She has been my best friend for four years." What an understatement. "Now there is this big hole in my life." In my universe. Travis was too depressed to even consider that his words might offend Austin. But it was common knowledge that no one was as close to Travis as Miley was.

"Look, I get that, alright." Austin's seeming understanding was very uncharacteristic. Travis snapped his head up to meet Austin's eyes. "But she has moved on. Some day in the near future, you are going to have to wake up and do the same thing."

That is what Travis needed to do. But it would not be easy. Travis had always pictured his future with Miley in his life. He couldn't begin to imagine it without her sweetly expressive face, her blond hair bouncing in loose curls around it. She was always twirling around him in some dress that she prattled on about what a great deal it was. And all he could do was smile and inhale as her perfume stripped off of her body and up his nostrils. That is how he would always picture her.

He tried to inconspicuously wipe a tear out of his eye as he toyed with the prospect of never seeing her again. He used to talk to her every day. Although she never seemed to realize it, Miley had been like a girlfriend to him all this time, minus the physical benefits. He had always held out hope that those would be added any day.

Austin checked his phone, as he constantly did. Travis remembered when he was little that his dad almost never used a telephone unless it was for work. Ever since they had become pocket computers, that part of life sure had changed. Men were clearly as addicted to using their phones now as once only women had been. "C'mon, man! You force me out on the town and then spend the whole night on your phone?" Travis griped. But Austin's face quickly lit up, his mouth spreading into a wide smile.

"Aw, dude. You gotta check out this video Tommy just sent me," he guffawed.

"No man, no more sports videos of guys getting nailed in the nuts."

"No, no. This is a sex tape! Tommy says the girl is even local. It is all over the Internet. Didn't say who, though."

At that, Travis ripped the phone out of Austin's hand. He protested, but didn't immediately attempt to retrieve it. It seemed he wasn't finished ogling yet. But a giant, nauseous knot was already forming in Travis's stomach.

Sex tape.

Internet.

Local girl.

These words echoed in his head as he watched the low-light video on the 5.5 inch screen of his friend's phone. The bar was way too noisy to hear any audio, and Travis was now glad of that as an angel's stoned face hungry for sex, her hair in disarray, came into view.

This wasn't at all how he wanted to see her for the first time having sex.

The nausea was quickly being replaced by white-hot anger.

Travis tossed the phone back at Austin, never bothering to stop the video. Austin fumbled it, but managed to grab it before it fell. Travis stood up, making no effort to slide his chair back, causing it to tip and slam to the floor.

"Trav! Travis! Where are you going?" Austin shouted after him as he headed for the door.

Austin would figure out the why the video upset him soon enough.

MILEY

Kiley tried to call a few times. Miley replied to her by text with very short answers.

Miley: Im OK.

Kiley: Where r u?

Miley: June's.

Kiley: Did u know? Bout the vid?

Miley: No.

Miley: Not til 2day.

Kiley: R u still w/him?

Miley: No.

It rained. It almost never rained in California, as far as Miley knew. But she needed it today. Since she was a kid, Miley had always found thunderstorms comforting. It must have been four or five o'clock in the morning. It felt like days since Miley had found out about the sex tape. She had not yet slept.

It was rather fitting. It had rained on the first night she had met Mark and been in his car. It was back for the end of them. A light little shower to signal the beginning, a harsh thunderstorm for the violent conclusion. The weather was demonstrating how their relationship had come full circle. If only she had known to take the first rain as the omen that it was.

She slid the living room window open. It resisted like it had not been moved since it had been installed, then the building had settled around it unevenly in the years since. The cool air blew across her hot face, putting out the fire in her cheeks and eyes from hours of crying. The sound of the driving rain was like white noise that blocked out any individual sounds of the cars or people below. It made it harder to hear the thoughts in her head, which was a very good thing. It gave Miley a few moments of peace. She loved the smell of the rain falling. She loved the smell of the musty screen that complimented it. She loved the safety of being behind the screen, where any insects could not reach her.

While the streetlights and headlights and signs made it quite bright, even during the middle of a thunderstorm, there were still dark corners and alleyways. Her eyes focused on them, waiting for something to emerge from the shadows. As her eyes adjusted to the darkness, they played tricks on her. And sometimes, for a brief second, she would actually think she had seen something.

It was like this that she finally drifted into sleep, leaning over the back of the couch, with her head on her crossed arms on the windowsill.

29

Miley heard pounding at the door. She waited for someone else to get it. There were no other sounds in the apartment. Miley's stomach did a somersault as she wondered if June was still in her room. Then her brain kicked in, and yelled at her that that could be June at the door. She might have locked herself out or something.

Miley jumped up from her awkward position leaning over the back of the couch. Now warm, humid air and sunshine were streaming in. Miley found it much less desirable. She left the window as-is to answer the door and stop the incessant pounding. Her upper back muscles screamed in protest as she straightened up. She didn't even bother to check if she was decent before opening the door. When the whole world had seen your sex tape, there was no mystery left.

Miley pulled open the door, expecting to see June.

Instead, Travis stood in front of her. He looked bigger than she remembered, seeming to fill the doorway. He looked tired (probably from a long plane ride) and a little like he had been in a fight? The pocket on the front of his gray hooded sweatshirt was ripped. His hair was sweaty and sticking out in all directions. His right eye was swelling.

Miley thought for a moment he had come to yell at her some more, chastise her for her poor decision-making.

But then he smiled.

Miley couldn't help but smile back at him, while studying the blood crusted under his nose and at the corner of his mouth.

He stepped forward in a flash. Before she realized what was happening, his arms were wrapped around her and his lips were on hers.

Travis was kissing her.

She couldn't imagine why he was doing this, but now she never wanted him to stop. His unique Travis scent, a mix of pine and olive oil that she hadn't even realized she missed these past three weeks, filled her head. He pulled back, looking into her eyes.

Miley leaned forward and kissed him back. It was all the good parts about kissing Mark, but without all that yucky gross feeling the next morning. She felt the passion, how good Travis's soft lips felt moving against hers, the tingling, well, everywhere. With Mark, Miley had to hold tight to the pleasurable sensations to justify the emptiness she felt the next day when her conscience was telling her Mark didn't have the same feelings for her.

But this was Travis! Good, sweet, sexy—SEXY?

Why hadn't she seen it before?

Travis.

His arms were enveloped around her so tightly she could barely breathe. As their tongues explored each other's mouths, Miley could taste blood in his. She pulled away.

"Were you in a fight?" Miley blinked her eyes as they became accustomed to being open to the light, in order to give her a better look at him.

"Yes."

"When?"

"Just before I came here. But I got a little lost. So, maybe an hour ago," Travis answered casually, checking the current time on his phone he had pulled from his back jeans pocket.

"Who beat you up?" Miley asked.

"Why do you assume someone beat ME up?" Travis said, obviously offended.

"Because you look horrible."

"Well, you should see the other guy. On second thought, please don't ever see him again."

"Who did you beat— Oh my God. You beat up Mark, didn't you?"

"You can thank me later," he said, smiling an impish grin.

"But he is an actor. He needs his face for his work... And he is an asshole. Thank you," Miley said, exhaling as she realized what she was saying.

"You're welcome," Travis stated.

"How did you find me?"

"I got it out of that a-hole."

"Oh, come in. Let's get some ice on that eye," Miley instructed.

"Aren't you going to ask?" Travis said, smiling a goofy grin.

"Ask what?"

"Why I defended your honor? Why I kissed you?"

"No." Miley didn't look at him as she entered the kitchen, opening the refrigerator door. She found carrots in the freezer, the bag coated in a thick layer of frost.

"Why?" Travis asked.

"Because I don't want to make you mad, like on the phone. Now that you are here, I don't want you to leave." She handed him the bag from the freezer.

"I am not leaving without you. I love you, Miley."

Now Miley could not resist looking at him any longer. She wanted so badly right now to believe that someone, anyone, could have true feelings for her. But why did it have to be Travis? The one person on this planet she cared about more than herself.

"I'm sorry," she said, tears coming to her eyes.

"I tell you that I am in love with you, and you tell me you're sorry?" Travis said, uncomprehending. He sat the carrots behind him onto the kitchen counter.

"I'm sorry, but I am not good enough for you to love."

"What?! Is that some bullshit he told you? Because I swear to God I will go over there and pound him again."

"No, no. It is simply what I discovered about myself out here. I abandoned Kiley, Jane, my mom, Jenny, and most of all you, to chase fame with a big loser with a big house. You are good, Travis. You have the purest heart of anyone I have ever known. You deserve the best. That's not me..."

"But do you love me?"

"That's beside the point." Miley shrugged and turned away, but Travis grabbed her arms and spun her to face him again. He pulled her chin up so that he could see her eyes. They were full of tears. "Yes. Longer than I have realized, I think. But that doesn't mean it is right. When we get back home, I am going to scour the state of Alabama to find you the perfect woman. I will not leave any bridesmaid unturned in my quest to find you—"

"I already found her." Travis kissed her again. She knew she should pull away. She didn't want to hurt him later. Instead, she melted into his arms. It felt safe there. She realized now that is what had always drawn her to Travis's arms, even when she had believed it was strictly platonic. She didn't know he was capable of beating up assholes for her. That was not a quality she knew he possessed—and it was kind of hot.

"How long have you felt this way?" Miley asked him.

"Too long," he answered.

"Why didn't you say anything sooner?"

"Because I didn't want to risk our friendship. I was waiting for you to realize it. But then you decided to stay out here in California, and I was afraid I had lost my best friend and my love."

"You should write greeting cards." She smiled adoringly at him.

"Then who would look out for you?"

"Point taken."

All this joyous revelation was giving way to a horrible apprehension in Miley's gut. It came on like a mega cramp, and she actually doubled over in pain.

"What's wrong?" Travis's voice was alarmed.

"June."

"June?"

"We have to check on June!" Miley ran over to June's bedroom door, still doubled over in pain. She knocked and hollered June's name, but there was no answer. The door was still locked.

"Maybe she left," Travis said, hopefully.

"She is a drug addict. You gotta get me in there!" Miley screamed at him.

He took a stance to knock down the door. In that moment, he looked more like an action hero than Mark ever would. And Travis didn't need a stuntman.

After three hard hits, the door casing splintered and gave way. June was lying on her bed, looking gray.

"JUNE! WAKE UP! JUNE!" Miley kept shouting at her and slapping her face. The slaps were bringing some color to her cheeks, but she was still unresponsive. Travis stopped Miley to check June for breathing and a pulse.

"She has a pulse, but I can't tell if she is breathing. Let's get her in the shower."

"Will that work?" Miley yelled to be heard over the blood rushing through her own ears.

"That is what they do on TV," Travis answered, already picking up June's limp body. Miley ran ahead to turn on the shower.

"Cold or hot," she cried.

"Cold. We don't want to give her third degree burns too yet!"

Miley turned on the cold shower spray. Travis sat her in the tub, half-propped in the corner.

"Make sure she doesn't drown," he bellowed at Miley.

"Where are you going?" Miley shrieked, panicked.

"To call an ambulance."

"But she will get in trouble."

"We can't handle this ourselves, Mile."

And she knew Travis was right. When had her dream vacation turned into an *Afterschool Special*?

Oh, right. The second she met June in the bathroom at the club.

30

Travis and Miley sat in the waiting room at the hospital, watching the televisions that hung from three of the four corners of the room. One was set to the sports network, one was set to the news network, and one was set to the entertainment network. They didn't know who controlled the remote controls and they didn't ask the elderly woman behind the desk. They sat there and watched as pictures of Miley and Mark attending the VTV Movie Awards together appeared on the news update every hour with the words "SEX TAPE SCANDAL" flashed across the screen. Usually one or two people in the room would realize Miley was actually sitting among them. They would stare. Then they would try so hard not to look her way that it was ridiculously obvious. The most recent stories said that Mark had checked himself into a rehab center for sex addiction. Travis said it was probably a cover story because Mark had to give his face time to heal before all the interviews he would have to do on his public relations goodwill tour back into America's hearts. What happened to June had really been no one's fault but June's. But Miley felt comfortable blaming Mark for it as well.

"You really beat him that bad?" Miley asked.

"Oh, ya," Travis smiled proudly.

"Trav, you are lucky he isn't pressing charges."

"Are you kidding? Then the picture of his face all pummeled would become public. That has to be the last thing he wants."

During one newsbreak, a woman sitting two seats down from Miley began to discuss current events with her friend next to her.

"I wonder how long it will before that girl tries to cash in. I bet we see her on the talk shows tomorrow. Or using it to start a career in porn."

"Oh, she could have a good one. In that video she does the Crazy Ghost, the Spinning Plate, and the Filthy Garcia."

"You know, when I first heard that story, I thought Miley Cyrus was the girl."

"That would have made it more newsworthy. Miley is a bigger star than Mark Tennyson any day."

On the extended entertainment newscast, they mentioned June's overdose. She wasn't a big enough star to be on every hour. The newscast even had trouble coming up with movies that she had done that people had actually heard of. One middle-aged guy in the room said, "Hey, I saw that movie. I liked that girl a lot. She was spunky." That would be a nice epitaph for her gravestone. Miley was just glad June wouldn't need it yet.

The doctors had pumped June's stomach. Her breathing and heart rate had stabilized. Now they were simply waiting for her to wake up. They had already talked to the cops. Due to the Good Samaritan law, June wouldn't have to do any prison time, even though she had a previous drug arrest on her record. She would have mandatory rehab straight from the hospital. June wouldn't be happy about that. June's roommate Kate was pissed that the paramedics had come to the apartment. Apparently she had something illegal she was hiding in the apartment as well, but whatever it was, it was not discovered. So Kate wasn't really as holier-than-thou as she pretended to be, looking down her nose judging Miley and June for their drug use.

Once they were able to talk to June, they went back to her apartment. Neither Travis nor Miley had anywhere else to stay in this city. Travis asked Miley how soon he could take her home.

"One more day, OK? I want to be here for June. Just a little longer. While I can be," Miley said.

Travis accepted that, but still went ahead and booked their airline tickets for tomorrow night. He said he didn't want to stay in this city any longer than he had to.

31

Miley wanted to be seen by millions of eyes and for everyone to know her name. As if wished to a genie from a magic lamp, her wish had come one hundred percent true, with unforeseen consequences. Miley and Travis had been home for a week. Miley felt lost in her own life. She had talked to Donna on the phone for a lack of otherwise motherly figures in her life. She had talked to her mother on the phone, who could only cry and say "my baby." Donna told her, "No one remembers the non-celebrity in those tapes. It is just fresh now, with all the talk shows babbling about it. Everything will die down. Then it will be known in history as 'Mark Tennyson's sex tape' with some nobody."

But it sure didn't feel that way right now. All the people who already KNEW Miley knew who she was and what role she participated in for the sex tape: willing victim to Mark's every whim. They would not forget her name to the sands of time, as Donna had suggested.

It was just as hard to come home and try to pick up where she had left off as she had feared. While Jenny had called over and over, leaving voicemails and asking Miley to come home and help with their business, now she probably wished that Miley had fallen into a fault line while she was out there.

When Miley had first found out about the sex tape, she had never even considered how it would impact her business. Miley's name and contact info was on the Pleasantly Perfect Party Planning website. Miley got hundreds of voicemails and emails a day, calling her everything from a whore to a hot mess to a sex kitten. Jenny got them as well.

One call even claimed to be from a group of porn stars doing a convention nearby and they wanted to hire her. Like she was going to believe that one. Why would anyone want to hire their company when everyone else was calling to cancel their services?

Miley had to listen to all the voicemails and read all the emails insulting her, so that she could find the ones that were actual existing clients' cancellations. Travis volunteered to screen them for her, but she declined. She was afraid if Travis heard all those things that the people were saying about her, he might change his mind about wanting to be with her. Although he had seen the sex tape himself, no doubt. Especially with the harsh review he gave to its creator.

There was another reason Miley did not want anyone else to screen the calls for her. Because she felt like she deserved to hear them all. Like it was part of her penance for her shameful act. Miley was still living by her new life slogan: I deserve whatever comes now. She hadn't told Travis this. He would be angry with her. He was still trying to convince her that she was good enough for him. She didn't quite buy that. She did love him with all her heart, but she found herself still pushing him away. She wanted to believe the sweet things he said. She wanted to believe that she was the person he thought she was. But in lieu of recent events, she simply couldn't make her heart commit. She and Travis had not even had sex yet. Did that mean their budding relationship was doomed before it had even started?

How was she supposed to give that part of herself so completely over to anyone else ever again?

Maybe Mark had ruined her.

"Wow, Miles. Didn't expect to see you back here so soon. Or ever," Keisha said. She was one of the servers that Travis employed on a regular basis. Miley wished he would terminate her. Miley found her distasteful and a bit immature.

"I'm just here to talk to Travis," Miley said coldly as she passed.

"Talk. Mmm-hmm. Ya, right."

Miley let the remarks get lost in the breeze behind her. She had much bigger issues right now than to let someone's suggestive comment, a person she did not even respect, regarding her new relationship get the best of her.

Travis was unloading his hot boxes from the truck. This was supposed to be a family reunion that he was catering, Miley believed. But she would have to skedaddle before the guests arrived. Just because her business reputation was ruined, didn't mean she should take down Travis's with hers.

He had his navy blue T-shirt with his company logo on with his black pants. He hadn't changed into his white dress shirt yet. She could see his muscles flexing through the material. His biceps were peeking out below the sleeve. He paused to wipe a hand across his perspiring forehead. Then he shook his head, so that his sandy blond hair could fall across his forehead again. How had Miley missed what an absolute dream gorgeous man he was? She looked over to see two more waitresses ogling him as well. They turned away before he could spot their admiring stares. Maybe they deserved a shot at him more than Miley did.

He started to head into the hall when Miley caught up to him.

"Hey, there."

"Hi! I didn't think I would see you here," Travis smiled widely. Miley couldn't resist smiling back at him. He was like an adorable puppy—whose naked body she wanted to bite.

"Well, I wanted to update you on the current status of our future events together." Miley reached into her bag.

"But you could have texted that to me," Travis replied, still smiling.

"No, I couldn't," she said, producing paperwork for him to take. "Here is the list of people who canceled both of our services," she said, handing Travis a single sheet. "And here is a list of people who are only canceling my services. They love your food, but you will have to get in touch to see who they hired as a new planning company, so that you can coordinate with them." Miley handed him four sheets of paper. Travis's smile suddenly vanished.

"So, all these people have cancelled your services?" he confirmed.

"Yup."

"This is like for three months out, some six months," Travis said, as he scanned the printouts. "How are you going to pay rent with no income?"

"I also have a ginormous credit card bill due any day. I have no idea." Miley threw up her hands.

"It'll be OK. We simply need to strategize a little damage control for you."

"I think my better option is to just apply for employment at Kiley's boyfriend's resort."

"But that won't open for at least another ten months."

"I know. I'm screwed." Travis extended his arms and Miley collapsed into them, a little more roughly than she intended to, but he still caught her. "People think I am strong, but I am not."

"You hide it well," Travis said.

"I just wanted the happy ending, you know? And everything got screwed up along the way," Miley continued.

"That is what we all want," Travis said, then kissed her. She tried to hold the kiss a second or two longer than she was comfortable with so that he wouldn't be suspicious of her doubts about her worthiness of him, then pulled away.

32

TRAVIS

"Hi Trav."

"Hi Miley. What's up?"

"Just sitting on my couch. Hiding from the world."

Travis's heart broke a little at the sadness in her voice. "Want me to come over?" he asked, reflexively.

"I thought you said you needed a good night's sleep tonight because you had an early day tomorrow?" Miley's voice sounded a little perkier.

"Well, I do. But really, who cares about being a well-rested professional, anyway?"

"Hee-hee. You do." Her giggle slowly died out to silence.

"Really, I can stop over...," he repeated. He was almost pleading for her to admit that "yes," she needed him. Or maybe he was secretly begging to come over, because he missed her. Because he missed the time they had spent together in LA, on the flight, and the first few days home, when it had seemed like they were inseparable. When he first kissed her, it was like his life could finally begin. And it had felt like she felt that way, too. But since they had returned home, she was pulling away from him.

Now he hungered to feel her, warm and soft, in his arms again. He needed to feel her lips pressed against his lips, his neck, his chest, his...

"No, that's OK," came her weak reply, snapping him out of his dirty daydream.

"If you are sure."

"I am. I care for you too much to let you make me the center of your universe," Miley said. Her words made him feel tingly all over. 'I care for you too much' she had said. He used to only dream of hearing her say such things.

"Miley, you have been the center of my universe since I met you."

"I know. But that was wrong of me."

"I let you," Travis replied, smiling.

"I know," Miley replied. He could tell she was smiling too.

"I heard from June today," Miley began.

Travis didn't like that the conversation had taken a turn away from their relationship. Although, it was possible the preceding conversation was more serious for him than it had been for Miley. "How is she doing?"

"She said, and I quote 'Rehab fucking sucks.' She says they won't let her have any fun."

"I believe 'too much fun' is what got her into the hospital with a pumped stomach and into rehab in the first place," he said judgmentally.

"But apparently she got in trouble in rehab for riding a cardboard box down some stairs. She sprained her ankle. June said it was only to try to get some adrenaline rushing, get a natural high. They said she did it to try and get some painkillers."

"It sounds like June isn't getting any better. What kind of place is it, anyway?" Travis asked.

"Apparently it is where Drew Barrymore went once. And Lindsay Lohan was there her third and seventh times in rehab. So, it is supposed to be a really good place."

"Hmm. Sounds like Lindsay Lohan might disagree."

"June says when she gets out that she is going to come visit me. That maybe she will just give up show business and become my assistant or something. Wouldn't that be fun?" Miley said.

"Fun," he agreed half-heartedly. Fun is not the word Travis would use. Miley talked highly of June, but Travis had never seen it himself. Miley said June was sweet and lively and always tried to cheer her up. While he had seen her, June was mostly in a coma or sick with withdrawal symptoms. This was the same girl who introduced Miley to the Mark A-hole in the first place. Miley still stuck up for her, saying June could not have known how wrong it could have gone. But Travis had an idea that maybe June did know.

Miley hadn't admitted it to Travis, but he was sure June had gotten Miley to experiment with illegal drugs as well. June was a bad influence. Miley still seemed so attached to this one piece of her California trip, like she wanted to prove to herself it had not all been bad. But it felt to Travis like she was trying too hard.

Travis also didn't want to remind Miley that she had no business at this time for June to assist with. Let Miley live in her fantasy, Travis thought, where June gets better and transforms from a valley girl to a country hick.

"So, what are you doing tomorrow after the shindig?"

"Oh, I don't know. I might stop by the house of this cute chick I know."

"Lucky chick."

"Ya, she sure is lucky to have me."

"Now, don't flatter yourself too much. Because you totally deserve it."

"Well, if I'm not coming over tonight, then I better hit the hay."

"Goodnight, Trav."

"Goodnight, Mile."

It wasn't a sendoff saturated in 'I love yous,' but it beat the hell out of the time she called him and said she wasn't coming home. She broke his heart with that. Having his thoughts gleam upon it now made him sick to his stomach. Travis hoped he would never have to feel like that ever again.

33

MILEY

Miley was lying on her couch, watching TV and feeling like a total lump. Where once her calendar had been packed with appointments with clients, florists, and caterers, she now found herself with free time on her hands. Even with all that free time, she still couldn't make herself unpack her bags from California. She had brought home so many new designer clothes that she had had to purchase two additional suitcases to bring them all home; some items charged by her, some paid for by Mark. Now they lay jammed into luggage, the wrinkles becoming more permanent by the day. She had only unpacked her underwear and toiletries, because she had to. Even a loser who no longer has a purpose in life doesn't want to sit on their couch without deodorant and clean underwear.

She couldn't read her favorite magazines or watch her favorite shows for fear her or Mark might appear in them. Such a thing was once her dream. How quickly a dream could become a nightmare. Be careful what you with for, and all that.

She no longer played the mental six degrees game, which had always been one of her favorites. The thought of how many actors, both top-selling and bottom-of-the-barrel, sleazy agents, and lothario movie producers who had managed to beat off while watching her amateur debut revolted her. She did her best to swallow the burning bile that rose from her throat.

She tried to shift her weight to her other butt cheek, but she met resistance. It seemed the couch cushion had its own idea of how her hiney should fit into the existing dent. She gave up and pulled the worn throw that was just a little too small up under her chin. She had the air conditioning turned up in her apartment specifically so that she would have an excuse to use this worn security blanket to make herself feel better. She couldn't pay the electric bill anyway, so why not go out in spectacularly irresponsible style?

Miley kept checking the time. Travis implied he would stop by after work this afternoon. She was really only killing time waiting for him to show up. She knew he would. He was good and loyal, like a Labrador Retriever. His hair was even the same color.

Miley looked at her phone. Twenty-five new voicemails. She had kept her ringer turned off since she got back to Alabama. But she still had to listen to them. Might as well get it over with now and be depressed before Travis gets here. Then he could cheer her up, and maybe she could avoid this unpleasant chore again until tomorrow.

She listened to message after message of people belittling her. Many of them talked about sex acts she had no idea what they were, but she had apparently performed them on the tape. Many of them claimed to be religious folks. Miley couldn't help but think, if that were actually the case, that maybe they should be at church on Sunday morning instead of leaving her upsetting voicemails. She was starting to recognize some of their voices. The same people were calling her over and over again. It had been three weeks. It seemed like there should be a new teen starlet/harlot to terrorize by this time.

Miley dutifully listened to each message until the end. She deleted the ones she had no business with. She wrote notes for the ones that she did. She mentally subtracted those accounts from the ones they still had, then splitting in half to calculate her cut. Things did not look good. Then she got to a message that sounded like an insurance agent or an IRS auditor; a serious tone that was all business. It was a woman's voice:

"This is Maria from the Rustic Glen Recovery Center. I am calling in regards to our patient Juniper Louise Mulligan. We were trying to locate a current phone number for her family. She called you often. We were hoping you might know how to contact them. Please call us back. It is urgent. There is no way to put this delicately, but June fatally overdosed last night. Any information would be helpful. I can be reached at 555-732-4922."

Miley sat there with her phone in her hand, staring at nothing. When she hit no button, the phone replied, "Message saved."

June. Dead.

It isn't like Miley hadn't worried about it. June had come close the day she ended up in the hospital.

But she was in rehab. She had a chance.

She could have left Hollywood.

Moved to Alabama...

...And what?

Nothing because it had all only been Miley's dream.

June had probably only said it as a joke.

Miley had taken it seriously, because that is what her heart wanted to hear.

Just like she had done with Mark.

She had believed he wanted her to stay in LA, so she had.

Now Miley's anger and hurt and sadness and hopelessness all swirled together into a tornado of emotion that overwhelmed her. She was mad at Mark for releasing the tape. She was mad at June for dying on her. She was mad at herself for believing in a fantasy that wasn't going to happen. She was mad her business was lost over some silly idea of love. She was mad that all this bad was clouding up her relationship with

Travis, which should have been the greatest thing to ever happen to her. And now it was overshadowed by death and destruction.

That is how Travis found her, curled up in a ball with her faded blanket sobbing on the couch. Travis was frantic to know what was wrong. He thought she was hurt. She couldn't even get the words out. She typed it on her phone for him:

June dead.

He kept asking if she had left rehab, and Miley kept shaking her head 'no.' She finally composed herself enough to tell him what few details she did know.

"How does someone overdose in rehab?" he asked, baffled.

"It happens all the time. Haven't you seen *28 Days* with Sandra Bullock?"

"Ya, that's a movie."

"It was based on a true story. I think... Anyway," Miley paused to sniff, "she is gone."

Travis sat and held her for a long time. Then he ordered a pizza and put on a movie. Miley was too distracted to watch. She had no appetite either.

After a while, Miley couldn't stand the suspense, and made Travis call the rehab back. She had no information to offer, other than she thought June's parents might live in Sacramento.

But it turned out the rehab didn't need Miley after all. The woman said they took June's cell out of her personal forbidden items hold box. While her parents' numbers were not listed, the facility called a few numbers in it. A nice young man named Mark something was able to give them enough data to track her parents down. They were going to have June's body cremated and shipped back to them.

Travis tucked Miley into bed. She protested, telling him she wouldn't be able to fall asleep and that she would only be able to think about June all night. But as Travis lay behind her, and she in his arms, she began to relax and drift off.

34

The next few weeks, Miley fell into a deeper depression. Bills started arriving in the mail marked overdue. Miley let Jenny handle all the remaining events without her. Travis tried to convince Miley to move in with him. He kept saying it would make sense for "fiscal responsibility." Who was he, the President of the United States? He said it was also because he loved her and wanted her close. But Miley knew the rest of that statement that he didn't say out loud. That he wanted her close so that he could keep an eye on her, to make sure she didn't do anything drastic; anything that she couldn't take back. So that she couldn't follow in June's footsteps.

She sat on the couch and hardly moved. Travis tried to draw her out to go shopping. When she turned him down, he knew her depression was very serious.

Travis would be gone to an event overnight, so Kiley stopped by to check on Miley. But instead of being understanding about why Miley felt like her life was over, Kiley told her to get over herself.

"I know what happened to you in California was terrible. But it has been over a month. It is time to move on from that and grow up. You haven't learned anything. You are still so emotionally wrapped up in the lives of celebrities, yet you are oblivious to showing any empathy to your own family. You are so concerned that Justin Bieber might suffer from some anxiety disorder or that Rob Kardashian is overweight and unhealthy, and possibly agoraphobic, but you didn't even care enough about your only nephew to call Jane and inquire as to how he is doing after surgery. I bet you probably don't even remember what the operation was for. It is like you live in this dream world inside your technology. It is time to wake the fuck up already. No one is writing your life for you. You are screwing it up all on your own."

Kiley could preach until she was blue in the face, but she simply didn't understand what it felt like to be violated the way Miley had. Just when she felt like her dreams were being realized, they had been ripped away from her. If Miley wanted to sit and sulk in her pajamas, who was she really hurting but herself? The earth could continue to spin outside her window. Leave her out of it.

TRAVIS

Travis had hardly been away from Miley, except for when he had to work. Tonight he had a late event in Burtonville, three hours away. He had already booked a couple of hotel rooms for his staff to stay over, weeks ago. Miley had asked him how he could make a profit that way. He told her it was all about getting his food out in front of the most people. Once they tried it, they would never forget. Then they would share that experience with their friends and family, who would then call him, generating more business.

Plus, it was kind of fun to put his employees up for the night. There was one room for the men and one room for the women. They slept on couches and air mattresses when the beds were filled. Usually someone bought some beer and pizza and they hung out and bonded. In the catering business, it's not like he could really throw his employees a company picnic. They were at those all the time—for other people's companies. And most of them worked other part-time jobs, many college students. So, this was Travis's way of rewarding his employees for a job well done. Usually he looked forward to these rare gatherings, where he didn't have to manage anyone, except for making sure they didn't trash the hotel rooms.

But tonight he was really dreading it. He wanted to get back as quickly as possible to be with Miley. He would have left everyone else and headed back, but he had driven the catering truck, and several others had ridden with him. He didn't want to leave them stranded. There was another car, but all those seats were accounted for. Travis didn't want to force anyone else to leave early on account of him.

This burned on Travis's mind all evening. It made for a very long night. He got everyone settled into the hotel. Everyone else participated in lively conversation. Travis called Miley. It was a short call. The thunderstorm outside was creating too much static in the cell signal to have a call of any length or importance.

Travis knew Miley was a big girl, capable of taking care of herself, but the angry storm somehow added to his worries. He stood at the window, holding back the tacky brown plaid curtains. The ancient rubber backing made a tearing sound, as if it had been stuck together for years, protesting Travis's movement of it. He watched the rain come down in sheets in the parking lot under the security lights. He looked into the black night beyond.

"You look like something is bothering you tonight," a petite girl with short black hair said from right behind Travis, making him jump. Her name was Cara. She was one of his favorite workers, because she was good at reading the customers and being empathetic to their needs. But tonight he was aggravated by her heightened perception.

"I would rather be with my girlfriend is all." As he said the words, he realized it was the first time he had ever used that particular term when referring to Miley.

"Missing her, huh?"

"Something like that." He couldn't have begun to relay all of the events of the past five weeks to her if he wanted to, which he did not. They were both quiet for a moment.

"She must be pretty special to elicit all this silent brooding."

"I am only worried because she is going through a rough time right now," he allowed.

"Then why are you here with your employees having a pizza party? Go to her," Cara said.

"I drove the truck. I can't leave people stranded," Travis said, his voice breaking a little at the end.

"I drove separate. You could take my car."

In that second, it was like the heavens shined down upon him.

"Really? You would trust me with your car?"

"Sure. But be gentle, she has a lot of miles."

"And the truck?" he asked, not thinking clearly.

"Bobby drives the truck sometimes. He can handle it." Travis knew this. He wasn't being a very effective manager. At the moment, he wasn't being a very effective human being.

"Oh, right. Ya. You'll let him know, won't you? And I'll get your car back to you tomorrow, I promise."

"Sure. Just glad I could turn your frown upside down," she confided.

"OK. Now you are pushing it," he said, smiling back at her.

She held up her car keys and let them dangle in front of him, like a string in front of a kitten. He snatched them, then crushed her in a big hug.

"Oh, you're welcome," she gushed, as he turned and was out of the hotel room door in a flash.

35

MILEY

Miley was awakened by knocking. She could hear Kiley calling her name from the other side of the door. Maybe she had come to apologize for being so harsh last night.

"Coming," Miley croaked.

She had been up late, not able to sleep in Travis's absence. She knew it would be a rough night, with him up in Burtonville. And the thunderstorm had kept her awake. She had nothing to do but examine the thoughts within her head. She didn't like spending time there. It was all dark and black inside. But now it was morning and he would be here soon, Miley thought, on her way to open the door.

"Miley?" Kiley's voice bellowed again.

"What?" Miley yelled back as she opened the door. She was slightly annoyed at Kiley's urgency. Had their mother lost her car keys at the mall again? But Kiley's face displayed a serious expression, which proved she wasn't joking around.

"Get dressed. You are coming with me now." Kiley studied the rumpled pink flannel pajamas with cupcakes on them Miley has been sporting for the last two days.

"Why? I don't want to."

"C'mon. I'm being serious. Get ready."

"Get ready for what? Is this an intervention? Because I am not going with you for an intervention," Miley said, half-joking. She didn't seriously think her family would do that to her. Would they?

"Travis was in a bad car accident. We have to get to the hospital NOW."

"How do you know?" Miley asked. Her brain did not even attempt to process the last sentence that Kiley had uttered.

"Small town," Kiley replied, walking past Miley and leading her into her own bedroom.

"But you don't even live in this town," Miley replied, confused.

"That is sooo not even important right now. We need to get to the hospital." Kiley started throwing clothes on Miley's bed for her to pick from. She simply stood there, looking at Kiley.

"I can't," she replied.

Kiley stopped throwing clothes long enough to look at her sister.

"Why the hell not?"

"Because if I have to go see Travis in a hospital, I might lose it. For good." She knew that wasn't really a cohesive statement, but Kiley seemed to understand the issue.

"I will go with you. I will hold you together. But we need to go now."

"No. If it is urgent, then I really can't go." Miley began to hyperventilate. She sat down on the floor, her back to the bed, and curled up into a ball. Her heart beat faster. Black dots swam in her vision.

"OK. New plan. Here is a jacket. It's denim. Denim jackets go with everything. Sweatpants, pajamas, panic attacks. C'mon. You are coming with me." Kiley made a grunting sound as she pulled Miley up from the floor, wrapped the jacket around her shoulders, and dragged her to the front door.

Once in the car, Miley sat with her head back against the seat and hardly made a sound. Two steady streams of tears made continuous rivers down her cheeks.

Coma.

Broken bones.

Internal bleeding.

Blood transfusion.

There was nothing that Miley had not heard before listed off on television medical dramas. Maybe thinking of it as part of a script would help. Maybe that could buffer her to the terrible reality.

Miley and Kiley were standing in the hallway outside the Intensive Care Unit of UniMedical Hospital. There were windows next to them. Windows that Travis could plainly be seen through. But she would not make herself look. At least not until Kiley led her through the glass door. Then Miley had to look up.

And she gasped.

Before her, Travis lay there almost unrecognizable. He had tubes and wire and monitors everywhere. He had numerous cuts and scrapes. His entire left leg was in a cast, along with his left wrist. All of his body not covered by casts or blankets or bandages was bruised, red moving through blue and purple on the rainbow spectrum. One of the IV bags hanging next to him was filled with blood, someone else's blood, now helping to keep Travis alive.

Sweet Travis. He didn't deserve any of this. His shaggy hair was pushed back away from his face, so uncharacteristic of how he wore it day-to-day. It was hard to believe he was still in there somewhere. Miley walked over to him and touched the back of his right hand; one of the few unmarked spots on his body.

"Why does everyone around me keep suffering? What if you are next?" Miley asked.

"I think Travis and June are two unrelated events," Kiley reassured her.

"Sure doesn't feel that way."

"Do you want me to leave you alone with him? We only have a few minutes until his mom gets back from the cafeteria—" This was important because only two visitors could be in the room with Travis at a time.

"No! Don't leave me, please."

"OK, I won't."

"I don't understand. If he is bleeding internally, why are they giving him MORE blood? It is all still in his body. What if they give him too much and he bursts?" Miley asked. She moved her hand from his, up to push his long hair onto his forehead. It looked darker as it kept accumulating oil, even as he lay motionless but for his breathing.

"From what the doctor said, his blood is all going to the spot of his injury. It is making a hematoma. Like an internal scab, I think. That can be a good thing, but it takes away from the quantity of blood available to circulate through his body. He needs that to heal," Kiley paraphrased what the doctor had told her in the hallway five minutes earlier.

"When do they think he will wake up?" Miley asked.

"They don't know. They actually aren't as worried about the coma as the bleeding. The coma will allow his body to put forth more energy to healing right now. But internal bleeding can be hard to tell how severe it is. They don't want to have to go in and do surgery if they don't have to, even though they already did some on his leg."

"His leg looks bad," Miley said. She looked him up and down again, picturing him riding his skateboard through the park, his blond hair blowing back to reveal his face. What if he never sat next to her on her couch again, laughing so hard that his beautiful robin's egg blue eyes were squeezed shut and watering at something she had said? "All of him looks so bad. What if he doesn't make it, Kiley? What will I do?"

"He will make it," Kiley reassured her.

"You don't know that. And he declared his love to me, and I have been nothing but a giant loser since. He doesn't even know I love him back."

"He knows," Kiley said.

"BUT I DIDN'T TELL HIM! What if I never get to tell him? He is a WONDERFUL person and he will die without knowing that. That makes me a TERRIBLE PERSON!" Miley erupted into sobs. Kiley hugged her and tried to comfort her. "Where did this even happen?" Miley sobbed.

"Last night, on his way back to Huntington."

"But... it makes no sense. He wasn't coming back. He was going to spend the night," Miley mumbled.

"He borrowed someone's car. He was coming back to see you," Kiley explained.

"But the storm was so bad." Kiley nodded. Miley continued, "So it really is my fault he is in this situation."

"No, it's not, Miley. He is a grown man. He made his own decision. He wouldn't want you blaming yourself for this."

"I don't know what I'll do if he dies."

"He is not going to die."

"You have to say that, you are my sister."

Kiley didn't respond.

36

The next day Travis's condition remained unchanged. Miley mostly stayed functioning by not thinking too deeply about any one matter. She wasn't hungry. But if she didn't eat, she found she felt worse. So, she made herself eat. She would count the hours on the clock until it had reached the pre-planned time that she had designated for eating. Then she would head to the cafeteria. The anxiety in her that was relieved from being out of the Intensive Care room was always immediately replaced with the uncertainty of what may happen with him while she was away. Then she would return to find there was no change in his condition.

She hadn't left the hospital since she got there, although Kiley did bring her clothes so that she could change out of her pajamas. Miley could only stand to spend small amounts of time in Travis's room, looking at him in that condition. She occupied her time trying to find all the amenities. She found a shower she could use designated for family members of those in the ICU. She found every vending machine in the hospital that was not behind a door labeled "Authorized Access Only." One of them had a video game on it you could play for prizes. Sometimes a half hour would pass before Miley realized she should stop. She never bothered to find out where to collect her prizes.

Travis's mom came and went. She would always say that he looked worse. Miley would always comment that she thought he had more color. His mom would say it was only the bruises. She knew from things Travis had said that his mom had a negative personality. Travis's younger sister couldn't come because she was at college two states away, and she couldn't miss her classes or her job.

Donna and Evan stopped by, mostly to see Travis's mom. His mom and Evan were cousins. In Oakley, where Miley grew up, everyone was a cousin to someone else. Except for her mother and father, who had moved there, rather than living off the land for generation after generation.

Donna and Evan only went in to see Travis for a few minutes. They were visibly shaken by the extreme nature of his condition when they came back out. While Evan took a minute to talk to Travis's mom, Donna came and hugged Miley. Donna had always been a hugger.

"How are you holding up, sweetie?" she asked.

"Not well. How long do you think he will be like this?"

"Oh, I'm no doctor. But I'm sure he'll wake up when he is ready."

"I'm not so sure," Miley replied glumly.

"Why don't you come home with us tonight? You could get a home-cooked meal, some rest."

"No. I'm fine here." Miley didn't want to risk what might happen if she left Travis at the hospital by himself. She felt her being in the same building, if not the same room, brought him some healing powers.

"You have been through a lot in the past month or so. I know I am not as close to you as I am your sisters, but if you ever need to talk, just give me a call, alright?"

"OK."

"I mean it. You promise you'll call?" Donna demanded.

"Yes, I'll call." Miley agreed, with no intention of ever doing it.

In the silence after everyone had gone, Miley recalled the harsh words her sister had said to her while she was slumped on her couch. That had been the very same night of Travis's accident. A great cloud of guilt collected over her. She HAD been neglecting the people she should be paying attention to, the ones who interacted with her in her life. Her television/computer/cell screens were not a window. They were a wall, to a world that would never be hers, one that she no longer wanted to be a part of anyway. But how could she move on? A lifetime of her brain concentrating on thinking one way could not be rerouted and changed overnight. Synapses didn't work that way.

37

Miley slept for a few hours that night at Travis's bedside in the standard-issue hospital turquoise vinyl recliner that folded almost flat into some semblance of a bed. When she awoke, she studied his features. She examined him for the faintest movement. There was only the rhythmic, shallow breathing. She could find nothing in his appearance that gave her any hope that the Travis she loved was still in there, ready to emerge. This scared her, deep down into her bones. She left his room and went to pace the halls.

She had to find a way to heal herself. She had to be strong for Travis. Now was not the time to give up on herself, on Travis, on her business—on anything.

What Miley needed was a plan. No, she needed the perfect plan. Only one person's face popped into Miley's mind. It was a friendly face who had never been anything but kind to her. But it still felt difficult to ask for help. It created a tension in Miley's chest that she could not seem to shake. Miley had made big mistakes. The only way she could see to clean them up was to go big with a solution. She just needed to realize what that was.

At the first sign of sunlight, she turned on her cell phone and made a call.

While she waited for Donna, Miley went through her voicemails for the last three days. She made notes about the ones that were clients, and deleted the ones that were purely character assassinations.

When Donna arrived, Miley suddenly realized she was famished. They started their strategy meeting over breakfast in the hospital cafeteria. Miley ate a giant plate of pancakes and bacon with a western omelet and biscuits and gravy.

"So, tell me what's on your mind, hon?"

"Well, I think I need to start rebuilding my life. I want to be the best person I can be when Travis wakes up."

"That sounds like a wonderful attitude," Donna encouraged.

"And I know it has to involve improvements for me, for Travis and I together, and for my business. I just have no idea how to actually go about it. That is where I was hoping someone with all your years of experience could give me wise advice," Miley began, shakily.

"Are you calling me old?"

"Um, that didn't sound as good out loud as when I rehearsed it in my head," Miley stammered.

"Don't worry about that. All this started with that tape of yours. It's just, well, rehabilitating a career after a sex tape isn't something I have a lot of experience with. I think big cities have professionals who do that sort of thing."

"But working at the Diner and the bar all these years, you are an expert in small town gossip."

"Well, this is true... When you put it like that, it seems pretty clear to me. You need to do something to redeem yourself. Prove to people that you have still got it. Give them something positive to talk about."

"That will take care of the business, but what about my inner me? And my relationship with Travis?"

"You know, honey, both your self-esteem and Travis are linked to your business, in ways you do not even realize. And sure, you could get along without it. But I think the business will be easier to rehabilitate than you think. I think if you can turn that around, the other pieces will fall into place," Donna finished.

"But what do I do about it? No one wants to associate with me now?"

"You haven't had any new calls for people wanting to sign up after all this 'free publicity?' " Donna winked when she said the last two words. How could she always stay so damn upbeat about everything?

"No. Only cancellations and hate calls." Miley's thoughts swam.

"Well, that doesn't leave us much to work with. Maybe we could get some new events from local people who knew you growing up," Donna suggested.

"Can you believe I actually had a call from people saying they were holding an adult entertainment convention nearby and wanted me to plan it?" Miley laughed. "Who makes this stuff up?"

"Maybe it is for real," Donna offered.

"They even called twice."

"Miley. That is the event you need to do," Donna said.

"What? No. That is exactly the type of thing I should NOT be doing, if it is even real."

"It is the perfect way to acknowledge what happened and what people are saying about you. Then you show them that you can turn it all to your advantage."

"I don't know—," Miley said, shaking her head.

"Miley, you asked for my advice. Now, I am giving it. Call those people and get more information. Book that event."

"Jenny is part owner. She might not like it."

"No, but I bet Jenny likes to have customers," Donna preached.

"Point taken," Miley agreed.

Miley headed back up to see Travis after her long talk with Donna. She approached the glass door, feeling the familiar dread. She pushed it open. Her eyes reflexively looked around the bed and at the chairs, to see if anyone else was in the room. No one was. That is why Miley jumped when she heard the voice, rough and gravely, speak her name.

"Mi-ley?"

"Oh my God! Travis, you are awake!" She stood there, hovering in surprise between the door and his bed.

"What happened?" he croaked.

Miley ran to the door, opened it, and shouted into the hallway.

"Doctor, nurse, anybody! He's awake, he's awake. Oh God! He's awake."

She ran back in and ran up to Travis, intending to hug him. But she stopped short when she realized he was still very much attached to all the same tubes and wires of the last three days. So she grabbed his good hand and kissed his forehead passionately.

Travis was trying to ask her questions, but he had to give up when the medical professionals came in and started asking him their own questions. Miley backed away to let them assess him.

"What is your name?"

"Travis Aaron Masen."

"Do you know where you are?"

"I'm guessing a hospital."

"What is your birthday?"

"March 25th."

"What is the last thing you remember?"

"I was in a hotel room, talking to Cara…"

"Do you remember the accident?"

"No. But it must have been a big one, because I feel like hell."

"Oh, Travis! It is so good to have you back," Miley said behind them. The expression on his face said he was confused why she was happy that he was in pain. "You were in a coma. For three days," she explained.

"Am I going to be alright?" he asked Miley, then looked at the doctors surrounding him, realizing they probably had a more knowledgeable answer.

"Your H and H has stabilized, so that means the internal bleeding has slowed." Satisfied that his consciousness was not a temporary condition, they all began to file out of the room.

"Internal bleeding? What the fuck did I do to myself?" he squeaked the swear word out of his body, but his words had more emotion to them than all the others had since he woke up. He was starting to sound more like his old, jovial self, even if it was merely a glimpse between the beeps of his monitor.

"If your numbers hold and you continue to show signs of alertness, we could have you moved out of the ICU by tomorrow," a random doctor said as he departed.

Travis stared after them, still puzzled.

"Can you maybe tell me what is going on?" he asked.

"Oh, Trav. I thought you were going to die. I was so lost without you. I love you," Miley's words fell out of her mouth, tumbling over one other.

"Was I going to die?"

"The doctors were worried about the internal bleeding, not the coma. But it sounds like that is better," Miley gushed cheerfully. Travis made an unhappy expression.

"What about my leg?" he said, motioning to the cast.

"Oh, it's still there," Miley said happily.

"Thanks for all the info," Travis said sarcastically.

"I'm just so glad you woke up."

"So, you managed to survive three days without me?"

Miley understood the implication in his question. "Yes. But it was very hard."

"That's funny."

"Why is that funny?" Miley asked.

"Because I was trying to get home to you."

"I heard something like that."

"I was worried you couldn't make it one night. That's why I was coming back early." He smiled a lopsided grin at Miley. Her heart nearly burst with joy. "What happened after that?" Travis requested.

"The cops said you were speeding and slid off the road in the rain. The car rolled, and hit a tree. You were thrown from the car at some point, which was good, because it caught on fire after that... Where did you get a car from?"

"Oh my God, the car..."

"What?"

"It was Cara's."

"You are so lucky to still be here," Miley said, tears filling her eyes.

"I haven't had time to process, but I am starting to think that."

"Trav—"

"Yes."

"I love you, with all my heart, forever. All this," she motioned at the monitors, "has been a big wake-up call. I want you to know I'm not going to feel sorry for myself anymore. I am going to be ecstatically happy that I still have you shining in my life." Her words caught on a sob in her throat at the end of her announcement.

"Thank you. I love you, too," he paused. "I don't feel much like shining right now. Can you call one of the nurses back in here? I hurt so bad. Maybe she can give me some meds?" Travis grimaced in pain.

"Oh, of course."

Miley was dying to tell him about her new plan. But once he had more meds, he fell asleep quickly. It seemed like a shame to make someone who was freshly awakened from a coma so drowsy again so quickly.

Travis's mom thought the same thing when she came in to find him already asleep again. She grumbled about taking time off from a new job to come and see him awake. She did nudge him until he was able to mumble to her how sleepy he was. Satisfied that she had gotten some reaction, she went back to work, only to return again at the end of the day.

Miley was thrilled beyond belief and scared at the same time. Somehow she had expected that when Travis woke up, that would be it. He would just wake up and walk out of the hospital back home, but he was still bandaged and in a lot of pain. It seemed it was merely another way that Miley's brain was creating its own illusion of reality. He still had a long way to go.

38

It turned out that the porn industry was like every other industry. They liked to have conventions once a year. They liked to get together and sell products, drink, and have sex. Well, Miley didn't know about the last one. Would that be considered working while on vacation for them?

Charlotte was the main contact for Miley to discuss details with for Xcitement Xhibition. The organization had been planning the convention for Atlanta, Georgia, the next state over. Then plans with the hotel and their former planner had fallen apart. That is when Charlotte heard Miley's story on the news, and decided to see if she would be interested in helping. Charlotte was very honest with Miley. She knew not everyone would jump at this kind of job. In fact, finding someone was proving difficult and the event date was drawing near. But she also suspected that Miley would have a lot of free time on her hands at this moment to take over a last minute project this large. Jenny kept saying no when Miley proposed they take the job. That is, until she heard how much potential profit they could make over the three days of the convention. Then Jenny was all in.

Since there were so many people arriving for it, the guests would be directed to stay at the two biggest hotels in Huntington. The actual event would be at the convention center, Shark Attack Energy Center. They were all lucky that it was available that weekend. While Miley felt guilty spending less time at the hospital with Travis, she had never felt more alive.

She had reason to get out of bed again!

The meetings with some of her suppliers were rough, and she knew it was because of the sex scandal. But Miley knew she had a job to do and wasn't going to let their attitude deter her. They weren't there. They couldn't understand how the relationship had flourished so quickly, and crashed and burned the same way. If she couldn't get a contract with her usual supplier for the best price, then she would go to the second cheapest. It wasn't an ideal situation, but it was still workable to obtain everything they needed to hold the convention.

Miley had been blind at the time, but now she could see how all the puzzle pieces fit together. She had only been allowed admittance to Mark's table at the club when he found out what movie she was involved with. He had asked her specifically that night about its director. Mark had expressly mentioned the movie set in regards to meeting Kiley. He had mentioned a CIA movie he wanted to star in, then proceeded to grill Jack about his next "spy thriller" project. He had targeted Miley for her connection to Jack Kahn. Kiley had been able to pick up on that within minutes of meeting Mark. June had all but confirmed it.

It didn't matter now, anyway. Miley had read that Bobby got that part. Maybe that explained their competitiveness as well. There are only so many big-budget action film roles to go around in Hollywood. Mark knew that opportunity was slipping away every day that Bobby was on the set of *Shoes* working with Jack, building a working relationship. That is why Mark had been so eager to try and get the Vancouver job. He was desperate for a big role as soon as possible. Vancouver was a last-ditch attempt which had also not panned out.

If Miley was honest with herself, she wasn't sure she would have done anything differently with Mark. She had been so drawn in by him. But it must have been all an illusion inside her head. Mark had turned out not to be so different from the guys at home after all, always wanting something from her. Except that he had a sports car and maid. Her mind had fooled her again, like so many other times in her life. It had been quite the ride, even if the rollercoaster did crash and burn at the end.

39

"Thanks for coming with me, Jane," Miley said. "Travis mostly sleeps because they have him so highly medicated for pain. I am sick of watching marathons on VTV and the classic sitcom channel."

"No problem. Anytime I can get away from a three year old seems like a vacation," Jane replied. Her long blond ponytail swung behind her head as she walked. She had on her usual oversized hoodie and mom jeans. Despite being a mom, there was a good figure buried under all that somewhere. "Plus, I haven't gotten to see you much since you got back. You can catch me up on your trip. You know, I mean the parts that weren't aired on OMGz."

"Those moments WERE most of the vacation."

Travis had been moved out of the ICU. He could now have more than two visitors at a time. Miley pushed open the door to Travis's room. His mom was there. Travis happened to be awake right then. His mother probably woke him up. She was prone to doing things like that, not realizing how much sleep helped him to heal. Travis always described her as a "hard woman to love," but she had always been kind enough to Miley.

As the two of them entered the room, Travis and his mother both looked up to see what the intrusion was, expecting another doctor or nurse. Travis's mother's face wore its usual look of negativity. But upon seeing Jane, it turned red and her eyes absolutely burned with anger.

"What is SHE doing here?" she bellowed.

Miley was shocked. Why shouldn't she be here? She was Travis's girlfriend, albeit very recently. But she quickly caught on to the fact that Travis's mother was not staring at her, but BEHIND her. At Jane.

Miley turned to look at Jane, who looked like she was about to cry. This was not the first time they had met, to be sure, but Miley could not figure out this hostile reaction, especially toward Jane. Jane had never hurt a fly. Well, except for actual flies, because she hated bugs. If anything, his mother should hate Miley, whose athletic prowess was on display for anyone who had a 5Mbs or higher Internet connection.

"This is my sister, Jane. She came along to visit today," Miley said, answering the question that she didn't know was rhetorical or not.

"I know her name. I know exactly who she is. I was there when she was born."

Jane seemed to snap out of her paralyzing shock now and found her voice.

"Miley. I'd like you to meet my birth mother, Connie Tucker."

"Connie MASEN. I did get married."

"But that is Travis's mom..." Miley told them both information that they all knew.

"Jane is my sister?" Travis had been quiet up until this point, but now he was trying to make sense of this conversation through his haze of painkillers.

"She is NOTHING to me," Connie said. She got up, clutching her purse, and charged straight for the door. The sisters backed up out of the doorway to allow her to storm out of the room.

"Wait, what?" Miley said. Her brain hurt from trying to sort all this out. "Wait. So Travis's mom is also your mom?"

"I knew who my birth mom was. I didn't know she was also Travis's," Jane relayed through tears in her blue eyes, trying to control herself.

"And I knew Travis was a second cousin to Wade, as are you. How did we all miss this?" Miley posed.

"Not enough family reunions," Travis kidded, trying to lighten the atmosphere of the room.

"I knew I had a half-brother and sister. I saw them—you—at Donna and Evan's wedding. But your mom was so hostile that I didn't want to dig into it any deeper. I never knew your names. She is already so angry that I even exist. I didn't want to make it worse."

"All I remember about that wedding was that my mom made us leave early," Travis said.

Jane pointed at herself.

"All I remember is the tornado," Miley chimed in.

"Wow. Mom sure can keep a secret. I am definitely going to have to find out more about this."

"Don't. It will just make her hate me more," Jane said.

"Jane, you are like the nicest person I know. If she has a problem with you, it is her problem. Mom can be a real bitch. Welcome to the family," Travis said, trying to flash a friendly smile toward Jane. He winced in pain.

"So, I am dating my adopted sister's half-brother and you both are second cousins to my twin sister's husband," Miley said.

"Kiley isn't married yet, or even engaged," Jane reminded her.

"Calm down, Miley. It is all perfectly legal. It simply makes our family tree look, well, like a bonsai," Travis joked, his blue eyes twinkling even in the unforgiving sallow fluorescent lights.

"A bonsai?" Miley was skeptical of where this analogy was headed.

"Yes. One of those little trees where they have twisted the trunk to look like a pretzel," Travis concluded.

"Makes sense to me," Jane replied.

"I think you guys are both nuts. It must be in the genes."

"You know, now that I think about it, you and my mom are similar."

"I'm not sure I like where this is going," Jane mumbled.

"Hear me out. Granted, I definitely haven't spent as much time with you as I have my mother, but from some of the things Miley has told me, things affect you both very deeply."

Jane managed a slight nod in agreement to his statement.

"It is just that in the case of my mom, she takes everything negatively."

"I think I can see that," Miley agreed.

Travis did his best to shift in his hospital bed, trying to use his arm that was in the cast to push himself up. Realizing that was painful, he switched to his right hand. A clump of his blond hair that desperately needed a trim fell over his eyes. He didn't try to move it, looking through it instead.

"While this family reunion is very sweet, I must interrupt to call the nurse and ask for more pain meds. If I doze off after that, feel free to leave. Jane, we will have to catch up more at a future time," Travis said.

"We won't leave. Get your meds," Miley said to him in a very tender tone.

"But you must be so bored hanging around here all the time. I'm fine."

"I kind of am. But if you were fine, they would boot you out of here so fast. Medical insurance companies won't pay for you to stay if you are well. So, the fact that you are still here tells me, that in fact, you are not fine."

"Are you going to play nurse when they do send me home?"

"I think I can handle that," Miley replied.

"Now, you will have to be gentle with me. Nothing that could rebreak my bones. Nothing that has been captured on video, at least not for the first few weeks."

"La-la-la. Don't want to hear any of this. My sister and my, well, brother. OK, I guess that is weird," Jane said.

"We shall conquer weird and eat its intestines for breakfast."

"You are the funniest brother I ever had," Jane complimented him.

"Thank you," he tried to mock bow to Jane while in his hospital bed. He winced in pain, then hit the button to call the nurse.

Miley leaned over, putting her mouth close to Jane's ear.

"I am a wedding planner. I have no idea which side of the church I would seat people on at my own wedding," Miley whispered anxiously.

"Your bigger problem: he hasn't proposed yet. You guys have been going out six weeks. Give him some time. A wise woman once said, 'Take care of the essentials, and the details will fall into place.'"

"Ah. That was me."

"No," Jane said.

"Had to be Jenny," Miley stated.

"Nope."

"Then who?"

"I heard Donna tell it to Jenny when she was planning Randy and Violet's wedding."

"Damn that Donna and her wise advice. So, all these years I have been jealous of your relationship with Donna, and I come to find out I have been running a business for five years based on her guidance." Miley shook her head.

"The world spins in crazy ways."

"And overlaps in crazier ones," Miley said, watching Travis as the nurse gave him a tiny white paper cup full of pills. He must be improving, because they had stopped administering the medicine intravenously.

"Don't get freaked out about all this. He IS your soulmate. You knew that in your heart before you even kissed him."

"Yes. You are right," Miley replied. She walked over to Travis's bedside and held his hand. She said something too softly for Jane to overhear, then kissed him. He laid back on the pillow, his face that had started to wrinkle with pain, already relaxing. Jane stepped out into the hallway to give them privacy.

How had Miley come so close to losing everything she had ever wanted when it had been right in front of her face all along? Miley began to cry now. Travis had drifted off to sleep.

She was glad there were no witnesses. Remembering the last time she had cried out of what she thought was happiness, in Mark's arms regarding the red carpet at the movie awards, made her cry even harder. How had she been so dumb, so naïve, to think that that was the ultimate happiest moment of her life? How could she possibly think that a handsome guy and a red carpet equaled happiness? Or love?

She had been a girl in lust, blinded by the cult of celebrity. Miley could see all that now—what everyone who truly cared about her had seen from the start. She had hurt so many people who cared for her by not listening to them. She had hurt herself most of all.

40

Everything was moving very swiftly for Xcitement Xhibition. It had to. Miley had been enlisted at the last minute and it was now only a week away. Miley really wanted to use Travis's catering company for part of the convention. The profit and the exposure would be great for him. Plus, he was the best.

Problem was, he was still in the hospital for a few more days. Then he would be home, with the use of only one wrist and one leg. He was in no shape to try to coordinate or cook for such a project. He said there was only one person he trusted to do his recipes justice and that was his younger sister, Taylor. She had been resistant to come while Travis was in the hospital. But when she found out she had a new half-sister to meet and that her brother needed help, she managed to make the trip for a three day weekend.

Travis was home from the hospital. Miley was staying at his apartment. He needed someone to keep an eye on him and he definitely needed someone to help him with making lunch and bathroom trips. Miley helped him take a shower too, which always caused unintended situations to arise.

Taylor was driving in on Thursday night. The convention officially started Friday night at five, although vendors would be setting up prior to that. Taste of Travis was providing the dinner Friday and lunch on Saturday. Miley was worried that Taylor would not be up to the task of cooking all that food. There was going to be three thousand people there over three days' time. Travis reassured her that Taylor loved to cook as much as he did. He was inviting over some of his top people to help to achieve the quantity they needed. With his supervision and guidance, he was sure it would all go smoothly.

Jenny was not so sure.

"You are letting your broken boyfriend, who is hopped up on all kinds of painkillers, cook our food. Food for the first full twenty-four hours of the convention! Are you taking his meds? Did you smoke some crack in Hollywood? This is OUR COMEBACK and I can't believe you are going to jeopardize it like this!" she yelled at Miley. She was someone you rarely saw raise her voice or lose her cool. That is why she was so well suited for this line of work, and for being a librarian. Miley was so surprised and impressed that Jenny had this fury of emotion inside of her, that Miley forgot to feel bad that all the hostility was aimed at herself.

"I hope we are not wasting time and resources on a potential disaster," Jenny said.

"As you mentioned before, this COULD be our comeback. He assured me it will all be OK. Travis's people are going to cover for him."

"Right," Jenny said, sarcastically. "We all know Travis is the backbone. Without him, it will all come crashing down."

"You don't know that," Miley replied.

"I do know that I am severely doubting your judgment lately, and I cannot live like this. If this event doesn't pan out, I believe we will have to dissolve our partnership."

"And if it doesn't work, I would totally agree to that."

"Hmph" was Jennie's only reply. Apparently she had expected more fight out of Miley. Miley knew this was a make-it or break-it event. That is why she was pouring everything she had into it.

Around 6:00PM, there was a knock on the door. Miley got up to answer it. No sooner had she opened the door than she was being hugged unbelievably tight.

"Um, hi."

"You must be my new sister," said a voice into her shoulder.

"Uh, no," Miley replied.

She pulled back, and Miley could finally put a face to the arms. Taylor looked younger than her twenty-one years. She had strawberry blond hair piled into a messy bun on top of her head. Her smile was huge. Miley saw no resemblance at all between Jane and Travis. But she could find some of Jane in Taylor's features, if she looked hard enough. Maybe it was easier because they were both female.

"New girlfriend? Sister of the sister?" she asked, hopefully.

"Correct," Miley answered.

Taylor squeezed and hugged her again. "It is sooo great to meet you! I'm Taylor, Travis's sister."

"Miley. Great to meet you."

"You guys have been friends forever. I can't believe I am just now meeting you!" Taylor gushed.

"Uh, I think I may have seen you at your high school graduation party, in passing." Which Travis, of course, catered.

"Oh, ya! God, why didn't I remember that!"

Miley knew why she and Taylor had never seen much of each other. While Travis adored his younger sister, he did not enjoy spending time with his mother. Travis had moved out on his own as soon as he could afford to, to escape her negative attitude and mood swings. Taylor had still been in high school, then attending community college, always living at home. Travis mostly stayed away. And when he did make a visit, he always did it alone. When Taylor did leave home, it was off to college too far away for casual visits, although Travis did ride his motorcycle over to see her from time to time. Owning his own business, he could make his own schedule and allow for such trips.

"Hello? Injured brother over here. I need a hug too. But not one quite that exuberant. I have broken ribs," Travis called from across the room.

"TRAVIS!" Taylor squealed and ran over to him at top speed.

Travis visibly flinched in anticipation of pain. But she did slow down at the last possible second.

"I AM SO GLAD YOU ARE NOT DEAD TRAVIS!"

"Um, so am I," he said with a good-spirited chuckle.

"I'm so sorry I couldn't come when you were still in the hospital. I had finals and work. Plus, you know how I hate hospitals."

"Yes, I know. I was glad you called though. You and Miley were both a good, positive balance to mom's energy. I couldn't exactly get up and walk away from her like I usually do. I was stuck in bed."

"And if you ever do anything like that again, my dear, sweet brother, I swear to God I will finish you off myself!" Taylor growled while beating him with a pillow.

"OK, MOM," Travis replied.

"You are going to mock the person with the weapon?" She flashed the crazy eyes at him.

"I'm sorry! Uncle. I swear I won't do it again." He raised up his hands in defense as he pleaded for his life.

"You better not. I hope you have learned your lesson about riding motorcycles now. I always told you they were too dangerous," she added.

"But I wasn't on my motorcycle."

"You weren't?"

"No. I borrowed a car from a friend that night."

"You did ALL this damage to yourself IN A CAR?"

"Yup. I have talent."

"What about that friend's car?"

"We are working something out."

"Remind me never to loan you MY car," Taylor replied.

"Are you ready to cook for the whole time you are here?" Travis asked.

"I will answer yes, but hope that you are kidding."

"You can hope all you want to. It isn't going to change the fact that I can't stand for long periods of time or use my left wrist."

"Don't I get any helpers?"

"Sure. They will be along later," Travis explained.

"Man, how do you cook so much food in such a small kitchen?" she asked, peeking in.

"Determination. And mad skillz."

"So when do I get to meet my new sister?"

"Jane will be coming by later. She has a three-year-old son, so technically you are a half-aunt now, too," Miley told her.

"Oooh!" Taylor squealed. She hit Travis on the arm without the cast. "You left that part out!"

41

Later, when Taylor was in the kitchen and Miley and Travis had a minute alone, Travis asked, "So, what do you think of my sister? And don't be honest. I want to hear only positive things."

"She seems really friendly. I'm a little worried she is going to rebreak your bones though."

The sound of metal against metal could be heard as Taylor shuffled pans in the kitchen.

"Ya, me too... Are you saying I am not friendly?"

"No, you are. But that is what surprises me. How can you and Taylor be so outgoing when your mother raised you differently from that?" Miley asked.

She was seriously curious. She was always trying to figure people out. If she had gone to college, maybe she could have majored in psychology. It still chewed at her how Mark could treat her the way he had. He had played her. But, seeing as she knew almost nothing about his past or family, her speculating always lead to a dead end. She was better off now, with Travis, anyway. But sometimes at night, before she drifted off to sleep, it nagged at her how a person could so easily expose something so private about another person. Maybe he was simply that open about his sexuality. But more likely, she had underestimated his thirst for fame; and, in turn, her own as well.

"Overcompensating, I guess. We realized early on that while not everyone deserves kindness, you don't get anywhere by assuming that no one does."

"Wow. You are wise beyond your years, Travis Masen." She looked at him with awe.

He sighed, throwing his good hand into the air. "I have been trying to tell you that for years."

"There were lots of other things you should have told me all these years, and didn't," she reminded him.

"But now we have a beautiful, long friendship to build on."

"Ya, and I can't wait for you to be out of those casts so that we can."

"Wow. I guess the videotape doesn't lie," Travis laughed.

Miley punched him on his left arm. "That's not even funny," she said.

"I couldn't help it! You walked right into it!"

"That's not exactly what I meant. Well, yes. I guess it was. It is just hard, because I didn't see you that way for so long. And now that I do, I can't help but want to... jump your bones. But due to the internal bleeding, the doctors said no physical exertion for a few more weeks."

"I guess I will have to settle for enjoying my sponge baths, for the time being." They shared a few kisses before Travis pulled away. "If I wasn't attractive to you before, what was I then?"

Miley had walked right into territory she didn't want to be in. She could never tell Travis the truth. That her brain had labeled him and put in an off-limits box so that she could only see him as a friend. And she wasn't even sure how or why that had happened. She knew Travis was waiting for an answer. The quicker she came up with one, the better.

Ah, she remembered now. It was because they were working together.

"We were working together." That sounded like a full answer, right? She kissed him again.

She had just become a partner in the business and didn't want to screw anything up. That included having a relationship end badly with the best caterer in southern Alabama. As they became fast friends, she had never re-categorized him. Which is weird, because he is totally her type—blond hair, blue eyes, not overly tall or manly or muscular. Although Travis did have a few inches on her in the height department.

Miley liked the illusion that she was a match for a guy, that she could take him in a fight. It was not true, of course. They had fought over cartons of ice cream and the remote control before. He could totally overpower her anytime he wanted. Most likely, even in his current state, although it would cause him pain and probably more damage.

Maybe Miley needed to take a good, hard look at her life and re-evaluate everything. What if her whole life was made up of self-deceptions such as Gay Travises and Marks who wanted her to move in with them? Maybe Miley being able to pull off this whole convention idea was also a misconception. That thought made her breath pick up speed.

Travis gave her a sideways glance. As her body was about to succumb to a full blown panic attack, the doorbell rang.

"I'll get it," Taylor yelled from the kitchen.

"No, you have to stay in there and cook!" Travis yelled, but she was already flying toward the door. She opened the door to two guys standing in the doorway.

"Ya, you are definitely not my new sister," she sighed, backing up and opening the door wide so that Travis could see the new arrivals from where he was seated on the couch.

"Luke, Blake. C'mon in. I'd like to introduce you to my sister, Taylor. Taylor, these are your slaves for the night."

"Longer, if you like, Taylor," Luke said.

"Knock it off. Either of you even looks at my sister, I will knock your block off!" Travis threatened.

"You and what army? You are kind of laid up there, dude," he replied.

"Nice to meet you," Blake said to Taylor, ignoring the others. "So, what are we doing tonight?"

In response, Travis got up off the couch, grabbing his nearby gray crutch and jamming it under his right arm. He couldn't use the other crutch due to his broken wrist.

"Oh no! If you are on your feet, that does not mean good things for us," Luke bellowed.

"You would be correct," Travis answered.

They all crowded into the kitchen. Travis, with his crutch and cast, was really more hovering in the hallway, looking in and directing them. Miley looked around to find him a chair to sit on and rest his sore body.

A few minutes later, the doorbell rang again.

"I'll get it!" Taylor yelled almost simultaneously.

Before anyone could make a move to stop her, she was climbing over Travis and the wooden kitchen chair he was sitting on to get to the front door. Everyone hollered in disapproval, but she ignored them. She flung the door open.

"OK, I'm sure you are not my sister," she said to the small pixie girl in the hallway with the short black hair and wire-rimmed glasses.

"As I am sure that you are not mine," Cara replied dryly. Her arms were filled with metal pans to put the food into.

"I take it you are one of my helpers?"

"I don't have a choice. By helping Travis, I am helping myself. I need all the hours I can get to save up for a new car. Since someone wrecked mine," she looked pointedly at Travis.

"Come on in, Cara," Travis invited.

"Hey Cara, you're late. Did you have car trouble or something?" Luke razzed her from the kitchen.

"Very funny, asshole. I had to catch a ride with a friend." Cara sat down the supplies and hung up her purse. She entered the melee in the kitchen.

42

An hour later, they were in full swing. Miley had been removed from sous chef duties because her chopped veggies were not consistent sizes. They had discussed getting pizza delivered to fortify the rag-tag crew, but Miley had decided she would pick some up when she ran the first load of food over to the convention center to put it into the refrigerators there.

The doorbell rang, and no one in the kitchen seemed to hear it over all the conversation and preparations. Miley walked to the door and opened it. A blond-headed boy ran in at top speed right past her without even looking up. Miley smiled at Jane, standing outside the door, bags under her eyes and hair escaping her ponytail.

"Did someone just let a dog into my apartment?" Travis asked.

Ethan barked from somewhere in the living room.

"Right height, wrong species," Jane replied.

"Hi Jane! Come on in," Travis yelled.

"She didn't bring more food for us to prepare, did she?" Luke grumbled.

"There is someone here who is very eager to meet you," Travis said, loud enough to snap Taylor out of her food-prep trance.

"Oh! It's my break time. Gang way!" she called, squeezing out of the kitchen once more. The others protested loudly.

Taylor tackled Jane with a hug before she even said "hi." And by the looks of it, all the previous hugs this evening had only been practice for this one. Ethan ran back in the room and began to cry.

"Let go o' my mommy!" he cried.

"He must think she is in real danger," Miley joked.

"With Taylor, she very well could be," Travis said.

Miley tried to console Ethan, while Taylor finally let go of Jane.

"Hi. I'm Jane. You must be Taylor," she managed.

"Oh my God! I have wanted a sister all my life! And here I had one that my mom was keeping secret from me. Not that Travis wasn't a great brother, but I couldn't do girly things with him like braiding hair and painting toenails," Taylor gushed.

"Ya, Jane never really did that stuff with me either," Miley chimed in.

"Let her enjoy her fantasy," Jane scolded. "In mine, my birth mother doesn't hate my guts."

"Ya, sorry about that. That's just mom being mom. She was bad before, and then when Dad left fourteen years ago, she decided to hold a grudge against the world," she said.

Ethan continued to run through the apartment as they talked, his little tennis shoes padding against the worn carpeting.

"So, what was your life like growing up?" Taylor asked.

"Normal, I guess. I was a nerd who studied a lot. I grew up with Miley, of course, and Kiley. They were the stars of the family. I sort of blended in, until I met Wade. Our parents announced their divorce one week after my high school graduation. I went to college, started working for Wade's dad, got married, had Ethan, found out I had a half-sister and brother. Now you are all caught up."

"Oh, there MUST be more to it than that," Taylor gushed.

"Ya, really no. Jane's life is kind of boring," Miley teased.

"Boring keeps me out of the media's eye," Jane stabbed back. Miley dropped the subject of Jane's dull life. "Travis, did you ever pump your mother for information like you were planning?" Jane asked.

"I did. Totally pissed her off, but I did get a little information. Apparently in high school she was dating some guy. He played football. She thought they were going to graduate and get married. She found out she was pregnant. She thought it would make him stay. But he went off to college without her. She gave you up because she hated that guy for leaving her. She hated everything having to do with that time in her life," Travis said.

"I figured it was something like that," Jane said, trying to be nonchalant, and failing.

"It seems to me she is actually mad at herself for getting involved with that guy. I don't think the anger has anything to actually do with you," he reasoned.

"I think the anger has to do with her mistake, getting pregnant, which is me."

"Right after that she married our dad and we came along. But that ended in divorce several years later. Maybe you should try to find your dad. Maybe he would like to know he has a daughter and a grandchild out in the world," he added.

"I am curious, but between you guys and Wade's whole family, I think I am going to wait a while. I think I have accumulated enough family members for now. More than I could have ever hoped for," Jane gushed.

"You know, I always thought Jane and I looked alike, but I think that was solely what I wanted to see in the mirror because we all grew up together. But you guys, sitting next to each other, really do have a family resemblance."

"You think?" Taylor wrinkled her nose and studied Jane's face.

Ethan ran by, screaming, making another lap around the couch.

"He is adorable," Taylor motioned toward the boy. "What's his name?"

"Ethan. He is three. I'm sorry he is so hyper. It has been a very long day. This is the wind up before the crash. It is getting late. I don't think he is going to hold up much longer."

"Oh, please stay a little longer. You just got here. Maybe you could be our taste tester," Taylor urged.

"I don't think so," Jane replied.

"Jane is a picky eater. I don't think she would be interested in anything we have to offer," Miley explained.

"I hungwy! I hungwy!" Ethan yelled.

"Well, looks like I have one taker. Follow me, big boy," Taylor said, getting up and heading toward the kitchen. Ethan ran behind her, his head bouncing off her behind when she suddenly stopped.

While Jane was there, the panic attack from earlier in the night held off. But once she was gone, it kept trying to creep back. When Travis was with her in the living room, she did her best to hide it. But when he was in the kitchen, she had a tougher time holding it together. Her breaths got faster and shallower. Her lungs began to ache from all the breathing activity which only resulted in a lack of oxygen. She couldn't help but think she was in over her head. And not even only with the food. She felt that way about the whole convention, her relationship with Travis, her entire life. She could feel each of these issues as blocks marked with clean, white adhesive office labels piling up on her chest like an evil Tetris game. Tears began to stream down her cheeks, only making the shallow breaths irregular as well.

The next time Travis started to leave the kitchen, Miley ran and hid in his bedroom. She didn't have faith that the skill set she had used previously to fulfill her planning duties was still foolproof. Assumptions on how people would react to varying situations had always been a benefit to Miley in her business. But trying to implement it in her real life had created disastrous results. Feeling ready to cancel everything, she called the one person who had made this all sound so right in the beginning.

"Hello. Hello?... Is someone there?"

Right then a big cry-infused snort came out instead of a greeting.

"Kiley? Jane?"

"Guess again," she mumbled.

"Oh. Miley, honey, what's wrong? Is it Travis? Do you need me to come over?" Donna asked.

"Not Travis." She took a couple deeper breaths. "I don't think I can do this."

"Do what?"

"The convention."

"But you have been working on that for a few weeks now. Is there something that didn't get done? Did something unexpected come up?"

"No."

"Then why the big case of nerves now?"

"All of a sudden it seems too big. Like I was an idiot to ever think I could take this on."

"Oh, now that isn't true. I do believe you are stretching your abilities further than you ever have before. But I totally believe you can do this."

"Really?" Miley squeaked.

"Did you just call to hear me say that?"

"Maybe," Miley sniffed. Her breathing was now more even.

"Oh girl, you have got to have more faith in yourself. You don't need anyone else to tell you what you are capable of. The same goes for the negative too. No one knows what is in your heart but you."

"Thank you. For listening and the pep talk and stuff."

"Now tell me, what are the next five things on your 'To Do' list?"

"Why?"

"It's a test. To get your mind out of this little rut you are in. Just tell me," Donna pushed.

"I have to take the finished food to the convention center and put it in their refrigerators. Then I have to label all the folding tables the hotel should have set up with their respective booth numbers. I have to post directional signs. Then I have to help all the exhibitors get settled into their booths. Then I have to do the final walk through with the fire marshal before the guests arrive."

"Then simply concentrate on those things and you will be just fine."

"OK," Miley replied. Even to herself, her voice sounded like it belonged to a little girl.

"But please tell me you are going to get some sleep tonight."

"I can't promise that," Miley replied.

They hung up, and Miley did feel a little better. Miley and Cara took a load of food over to the Shark Attack Energy Center in the catering truck. They stopped to pick up pizzas on the way home.

43

TRAVIS

God, I hurt. I shouldn't even be here. Working. I should be at home in bed.

Those were all things Travis told himself as he sat in the borrowed wheelchair. But he wanted to be there to help Miley. Or, more correctly, to be there in case something went wrong and she needed a shoulder to cry on. Not that he thought that would actually happen. And he REALLY didn't think that now that he had seen her in action. Miley was back to her old self. She was actually better than her old self. She was more determined, although she was used to only keeping up this kind of pace for eight hours at a stretch. She was going on twenty-four hours straight right now. He might have to tie her down and make her take a nap. I can't wait till I'm healed and I can tie her down for other reasons, he mused.

She was talking to people again without fear of judgment. She was in all her organizing, customer relations glory. She didn't realize a lock of her hair had fallen down on the side of her face, having escaped her updo. It was a lone ringlet. As Travis caught her eye, she had to look through it to make eye contact with him. She flashed him an exhausted smile before she continued talking with the bald man in the suit in front of her. Travis had no idea who the guy was.

She told Travis earlier that several vendors offered her a distribution deal on her video with that asshole Mark. She simply answered that she "didn't own the rights." Mark was now out of rehab for "sex addiction" (i.e. his ass whooping). It was a good thing he had whooped his ass before the car accident because Travis didn't think he would be as effective now. Maybe the accident was karma's way of dishing back to him what he had given out. No matter. Mark had deserved it.

Mark had started to go on the talk show circuit to apologize. How nice for him; keeps his name in the news. Poor Miley. It was just re-stirring the fire of controversy for her, which had only recently begun to cool down.

Maybe Donna was right after all. Maybe this was what Miley needed to find herself again; a project she could throw herself into. And this group was definitely not one to make a fuss about her previous transgressions. Travis hoped this would heal her from all the trials of the last several months. She could heal mentally as he healed physically.

Ya, Miley would be alright. When she looked his way again, he gave her a supportive wave.

"Hey man, you have a different set of wheels than when I saw you last. Must be cramping your style," Josh Tucker said, approaching Travis with his brother Wade trailing behind.

"Ya, totally. No idea when I will be able to get back on my motorcycle or my board again."

"How's the event going?" Josh asked.

"Quite the wares on display around here," Wade chuckled, his blue, attentive eyes absorbing all the displays of the nearby booths.

"I didn't expect to see you guys here," Travis said, bending his neck back to make eye contact from his chair.

"Really? I couldn't resist coming down here to see all the stars on display—" Wade began, before Josh cut him off.

"I came to see what kind of arrangements were going on here. Maybe I could hold something like this at the resort in Oakley next year."

"Oh, then we could get a backstage view—," Wade wrung his hands excitedly, before Josh interrupted him yet again.

"Shut it dude, alright! I'm trying to be all professional here!"

"Oh, sorry," Wade apologized, running his hand through his blond hair.

"You've already seen half the women in Oakley naked. Ain't that good enough for you?" Josh reminded his brother, annoyed.

"I see your point. But it's been a long time."

Travis found himself laughing at them in spite of himself.

"I talked to Miley earlier," Josh began. "And she said you might be interested in some space in the hotel. I just had a national chain drop out because they said they didn't think they would do enough business in Oakley. Douchebags."

"Real professional," Wade snickered over his shoulder.

"Yes, actually I would be VERY interested," Travis replied, trying to sit up straighter in his seat.

"Now, it is a pretty small space. If it isn't what you are looking for, I would totally understand."

"I would love to come check it out," Travis replied, trying to convey his eagerness through his exhaustion.

"Great! Here's my card. Give me a call when you guys are all done with this here," Josh said, motioning his hand behind him.

"Stop showing off, dude. 'Look at me. I'm important. I have business cards,'" Wade mocked.

"Will you zip it already? Behave or I won't give you a ride back to Oakley," Josh threatened, but Wade's eyes grew large and mischievous as the vision of that scenario ran wild in his head. "No. On second thought, I couldn't do that to your WIFE and CHILD," he emphasized.

"Are you sure you want to put up with his ass every day? I'm not sure it would be worth the hassle," Wade whispered loudly to Travis behind Josh's back.

"If it means steady business, I could handle just about anything."

"Ya, I heard you handled that movie star pretty well," Wade added.

"Hey, right here," Josh said, holding up his hand for a fist bump. Travis's fist met his. "We have to stick together and protect our women." Travis nodded. "We'll be in touch, alright?" Josh waved to Travis as they began to walk away.

"Sure. And thank you."

"Don't thank me yet. You haven't seen how much rent is," Josh finished, winking at him.

Travis watched the men disappear into the sea of people in the room. He wanted to plot out this new business development that had been dropped in his lap. But he was so drained already that it didn't seem like a possibility right now. He attempted to steer the hotel's wheelchair straight using only one hand, toward a back room where he could take his pain meds and nod off for a little while.

MILEY

The convention went off with no major issues. There were little things here and there, including a short power outage caused by overloading a circuit. But they all seemed to be resolved in a manner agreeable to all the major parties involved. Miley had underestimated the security needed to keep out those protesting for wholesome family values. But Charlotte happily approved the last-minute addition to the original budget to keep the peace. Charlotte was very happy to finally meet Miley face-to-face. At the conclusion of the event, she could not say enough good things about her performance over the weekend.

While the event had essentially been spread out between three different locations, many vendors expressed wanting to hold Xcitement Xhibition here again in the near future. Some of the stars who had come to sign autographs recognized Miley from her sixteen minutes of fame. They told her she had, to quote them, "mad skillz", both on tape and at making a giant party run smoothly. Miley took it as the compliment it was intended to be. Everyone said they would recommend her planning services, even though almost no one actually lived in the Alabama area where she conducted business. She only wished Travis was here to listen to the raves about his food. But he had stayed home today. He overdid it the previous three days. He was still mending from a very serious auto accident.

44

By the time the three day convention was over, Miley had had six hours of sleep and more Shark Attack Energy drinks than she could count. She went to Travis's apartment and did nothing but sleep for twelve hours. Afterwards she didn't even know why she had gone there. She was staying there to wait on Travis, but she was no help to him when she was unconscious. She could have gone back to her place. That, thanks to the convention, she could afford to pay the rent on again.

"Do you think you will ever do an event like that again?" Travis asked her as she sat on the couch next to him, and flipped on the TV. The local news flashed onto the screen.

"Do you mean 'Would I do another multi-day event?' or 'Would I do more events for the adult entertainment industry?'"

"I meant the first one. I actually began to forget what they were selling after a while. They were just people like anyone else. They were only trying to sell a product."

"I agree. That is, if you don't look at the pictures on the packaging too closely. Yes, I would do another big event again. But not for several months. And I would ideally have more lead time to plan and cost-cut for the client."

"Do you think you will get more business out of it? And, of course, by that I mean more business for me?" Travis inquired.

"I already have three more jobs lined up now than I did three days ago. Maybe Jenny will forgive me someday for all this trouble I caused," she said.

"Time—and money—heals all wounds."

The commentator on television began a new story:

Tonight there was a different kind of party going on at the Shark Attack Energy Center: Xcitement Xhibition, an adult entertainment industry expo. A group of pornographic actors and actresses from around the country gathered to meet and greet their fans. Almost two hundred exhibitors selling every kind of adult novelty and media imaginable were also on-site. Even more notable, Huntington's own Miley Riley, owner of Pleasantly Perfect Party Planning, arranged the festivities. She made national news recently, linked to movie star Mark Tennyson and involved in a sex tape scandal. You might say that party was right up her alley.

In tomorrow's weather...

"Travis—," Miley looked over at Travis, who was now watching the next story on the news. Miley's heart felt heavy. Her words got stuck in her throat on her emotions.

"Mmm." Travis turned to look at her more closely.

"I love you."

"I love you too, you know that."

"Can we start our happily ever after now?" It was a ridiculous question to ask him. Like he had any say over how Fate would find ways to screw with their lives. But she still needed his reassurance.

"Oh, I am ALL-FOR-THAT."

Travis smiled at her. She leaned over against him, lining her right side carefully up against his wounded left side. They looked into each other's eyes. Then their faces moved toward each other and they kissed for several minutes.

Miley thought of that poem that every kid gets stuck reading in high school. That one about taking the road less traveled.

Well, Miley had not merely taken the road less traveled. She had taken the pothole-riddled dirt road with a bridge washed out. Up a mountain. In a blizzard. But somehow, as she laid here with Travis now, she had reached her destination and found everything she was looking for. It seemed ironic, as she was just sitting next to Travis, as she had done so many times before. She was right back where she had started. But they were more to each other now. She knew now it was much more fun to watch movies than to see what really happened in trying to create them. She recognized that she had to reassess her assumptions often, to verify that they were true.

She had learned a lot about herself, and what she was made of. If she had taken the easy route, she would not be here right now.

Somehow, this made Miley smile.

EPILOGUE

They were all gathered in the circle drive that lead to the main entrance of the large hotel that was the heart of the Prestigious Oaks Golf Resort. The ribbon cutting would be the media's first official look inside. But of course all the Tuckers and Rileys had already been inside many times. In the past few weeks, it felt as though they were all living there as final preparations were completed. Josh Tucker stood up on the stage in a dashing gray suit. Miley was not used to seeing him dressed up. He faced several television cameras from the regional stations. Oakley, of course, was too small to have one of their own.

"I want to welcome you all here today for the ribbon cutting ceremony of the Prestigious Oaks Golf Resort. I want to take a minute to thank the investing group of JT and Associates, without whom this project would never have come to fruition. Most of all, I want to thank the wonderful people of Oakley, my own hometown, for believing in me and this project. Thank you for putting up with the construction traffic on the roads, and the customers in your businesses. May it continue!" Josh yelled the last sentence, to a round of cheers from the crowd.

"He worked all night on this speech. He was so afraid of saying the wrong thing and offending someone," Kiley whispered into Miley's ear. She stood next to Miley in a little black dress. It was just like Kiley to not even see the need for a little color on a day such as this. Miley was surprised Josh didn't specifically give a shout-out to Kiley in his announcement.

Miley had never seen Josh be this serious about anything before. At family gatherings, he was always the one cracking non-stop jokes, unless his brother Wade was there too. Then they fed off each other, and that only got them ribbing at a faster and more furious pace. Miley had always supported his idea of bringing more business and tourism into Oakley. Everyone in town knew the whole place would have become a ghost town twenty years ago if his father, Evan Tucker, had not used his resources to assist the remaining farmers.

But even with that, how long would the other businesses survive with only a handful of farmers to patronize an entire town?

While Miley had always believed in Josh's idea for a resort, she did not believe it would actually be completed. It was not for a lack of passion on Josh's behalf. But she knew that he had no experience in this area. She had been amazed, watching over the past four years, how by self-educating himself on the topic and picking the right experienced investors, he had made his ambitious dream a reality.

Miley felt a wave of contentedness wash over her, as the men making the speeches continued. Skip Wickley, long-time mayor of Oakley, spoke, and was followed by a local state congressman. Miley looked at Kiley, who had much more invested into the project than she did, as tears streamed down her cheeks. Kiley had heard nightly updates when Josh would come to bed, or a phone call saying he wouldn't make it home until late due to an unforeseen complication. Miley looked at Josh's dad, Evan, who always was so good at hiding his emotions. But today his time-worn face was beaming with pride. Donna cried with joy next to him. Jane stood between Donna and Wade, round with second child. Josh's other brothers, Randy and Pete, were also there with their wives and children.

Travis stood next to Miley's left. He was also in a suit and tie. To a stranger, his long hair clashed with his clothing. But with the sun glinting off his golden locks, Miley thought he looked absolutely sworn-worthy. He exuded accomplishment. He had a stake in all this too. The first Taste of Travis café was set to debut inside the resort. While there would be several other restaurants besides his, they would be more formal dining sit-down establishments. Being one of the only two carry-out food places in the building, aside from the vending machines, it is expected to be very popular with the employees on their breaks, especially his hot pita sandwiches. Who doesn't prefer a hot lunch to cold cuts? And even better when it is one you can carry with you without worrying about the delicious contents spilling out. Miley herself had organized and promoted the opening ceremony celebration, which Travis was catering the refreshments for as well.

Looking around her, Miley couldn't help but feel like this project's success was more than Josh's alone. It was a success for his whole family, for the whole town. For all those who were already moving to Oakley and building new houses for the jobs that now existed here. This was everyone's achievement to celebrate.

While the profitability of her party business was still not back to where it had been prior to her trip, it had recovered. Miley felt very fortunate for that. She had almost lost everything that she hadn't realized was so valuable to her. "I deserve whatever comes now." Miley turned the familiar refrain over in her mind like a rotisserie chicken. But recently it had changed for her, from a negative connotation to a positive one. Words that had been born out of the lowest point in her life now revived her with new meaning and hope.

Miley was snapped out of her internal reveling when Josh took the microphone once again. Hadn't he already spoken?

"This is already such a special day in my life. But I am going to roll the dice and see if I can make it even better," Josh began.

"Hey, you aren't opening a casino here!" someone heckled; Wade, of course.

"Kiley, I owe you the biggest thank you of all. Please step up here." Josh motioned for her to join him on the makeshift stage.

"Oh my God. What is he doing?" Kiley said to Miley, shaking her head as she began to move forward through the crowd.

When she had reached the stage, he gave her a hand to assist her in ascending the few wobbly stairs. He did not let go of her hand as he led her to the middle of the stage. Then he got down on one knee and reached into his pocket. He pulled out a ring box. He had to release Kiley's hand, then, to open the box and present it to her. She took that opportunity to put both her hands over her wide open mouth. Her eyes were bugged out in surprise. Travis grabbed Miley's hand and squeezed it.

"Kiley Riley, will you do me the honor of being my wife?" Josh asked. He looked very happy, and a little like he may vomit at any second, if those two emotions could be present at the same time on someone's face. Miley thought it was a good thing he was already down on one knee, in case he should faint or something.

"Yes." The crowd had to read her lips as Kiley said it very quickly, and with no amplification of a microphone. She got down on her knees to hug Josh. Everyone applauded. Cameras and phones snapped pictures. When they left the stage, Jane was the first one to hug her. Miley and Travis smiled at one another. Their congratulations would have to wait as they began to head inside ahead of the crowd for the final preparations for the celebration lunch.

After the grand opening festivities had been completed and cleaned up, Travis and Miley went up to one of the rooms in the twenty-story hotel Josh had reserved for them. They should have been exhausted, but instead they were giddy, riding the high of new beginnings.

Travis didn't notice Miley at first, emerging from the bathroom, as he dug into the plate of chocolate covered strawberries and bottle of champagne that had been left there for them by room service. Travis had removed his shirt and sat with his bare chest and toned muscles exposed, one of his legs hanging off the side of the bed, still in his black dress pants. But it was no match to Miley's exposure.

"These are really good. I prefer milk chocolate. But that is just me, I guess," Travis said, sensing she had entered the room, but not looking up. Then he did. "Holy mother of God. You look... Wow."

"Thank you. That is the exact reaction I was going for," she smiled coyly at him. She was wearing brand new lingerie she had bought specifically for this occasion.

Travis's eyes roamed over her body, hungering for her as she had only seen him do for a perfectly prepared steak. The black corset accentuated her small waist and put her average breasts on a lace shelf to better display them. She knew the long thigh-high black stockings drew his attention to her already long legs. She had put on her black, strappy high heels to complete the fantasy.

"I figured today was cause for celebration," she continued.

Travis got up and moved across the room to take her in his eager embrace.

"I like the way you think," he said, placing a hand on her neck to tilt her head back slightly as he placed his lips on hers, sliding in his tongue to possess her mouth. He slid his hand down her cheek, past her neck to graze her breast through the thin lace. When it was done with its dalliance there, he moved it ever so slowly down the smooth satin of her corset to rest on her thigh. He broke the kiss, reaching behind him with his other hand for a strawberry.

"A sweet for my sweet," he told her, and placed it in her mouth to take a bite. It was rich and juicy in her mouth. He placed it back on the tray, while his other hand moved down between her legs. As his fingers gently thrummed at the fabric, her heat intensified.

"It feels like someone is ready for me."

"I have been waiting all day," she cooed seductively, running her hand through his shaggy blond hair. Somehow the scraggy skater boy she had befriended had matured into a sexy man in front of her eyes. And she had almost missed it. She laid a slow, hot kiss on his lips now, moving her hand to unbutton his pants and unzip his fly. His ready cock, which was already stressing the seam, emerged, its hard length showcased through his boxers.

"I want you so bad, Miles."

"Then what are you waiting for?"

He picked her up, she automatically hooking her legs around his hips. He dropped her onto the bed. He ran his hands up and down the smooth fabric and lace of her corset. Then he grunted in frustration. "Ugh. How do I get you out of this thing?"

Miley giggled conspiratorially. "It has a side zipper."

They managed to unzip the garment and he started to slide it down her body. Miley quickly stopped him, so that she could detach the garters from the stockings first. His pants were removed as well. He laid Miley back, her blond hair splayed against the pillow. He looked down at her like she was the only woman in the world. Travis made her feel like a goddess.

He kissed her neck, then sucked on it, until her skin was between his teeth, pleasure turning to pain before he finally released her flesh from his hold. He did this in turn—kissing, then sucking, then biting—down her chest, to each breast and nipple, then across her stomach. In this way he took possession of little parts of her body at a time, but always with her permission, always giving them back before he took ahold of something else. They were sharing each other's bodies. Miley never felt like she had to sacrifice her feelings to be with Travis. Being with Travis wasn't a gateway to something more—being with him was all the prize she needed.

He devoured each of her thighs before dipping between them into her dewy folds.

"Oh God, Travis." Her body twisted with the ecstasy of his mouth against her throbbing clit. He raised up.

"Do you want me to stop?" he asked, teasing. His blue eyes danced in the dim light, his lips glistening with her own juices.

"Don't stop," she managed to say, a tiny squeak coming out at the end. He flicked his tongue against her fire and she went up in flames, squeezing his head between her legs until he begged for her to release him. Miley closed her eyes and tried to remember her own name as her blood pounded in her veins. A moment later, he was ready and eager for her. His throbbing erection stretching her, stoking her own heat.

"Travis, I'm so sorry."

"What are you sorry about, baby," he asked.

"I'm sorry for overlooking you for so long. You were always what I needed. Always."

He chuckled, moving in and out of her so slowly that she had to arch her back with every thrust, trying to get more of him. "You have apologized for that before. We have been over this. I wasn't upfront with you about things. Uh, ya," he shuddered as one of Miley's orgasms tightened around him.

"We are not going to bring all this silly old business up ever again, OK?"

"Oh, OK. Yes."

Their bodies moved in unison, him filling her. He completed her. He was the ying to her yang. Miley writhed under him, not able to control her body with so much pleasure coursing through it.

He let his chest rest against hers as he came down from his hands and gently stroked her hair. It was damp now from the heat of exertion, as was the skin on both of their bodies. Travis's eyes, wild with passion, his cheeks flush with effort, met hers. Then he leaned in and kissed her deeply. His mouth followed a trail around her neck to her ear. Miley wrapped her legs around his hips, allowing for deeper penetration. He licked her earlobe, then pulled the soft skin into his mouth. Travis whispered sweet nothings into her ear. This continued until he shuddered with his climax.

TRAVIS

"So, I suppose you are looking to get a ring on YOUR finger now," Travis began some time later as they stood on their balcony, his arms wrapped around Miley, both of them cocooned inside the same sheet off of the bed. He had everything he had ever wanted wrapped in his arms as they watched the sun sinking over one of the resorts' three golf courses.

"Of course, but there is no rush. I want you to have as long to save up as possible. That means a bigger ring for your fiancé," Miley replied.

"Damn. I forgot you are the gold digging sister," he joked.

"Well, then it is a good thing that I reminded you." She bumped his shoulder playfully with her own. "Plus, it wouldn't be much of an improvement in the name department," she continued.

"What's wrong with my name?" Travis accused.

"It's not your name, it's mine. I would be giving up rhyme for alliteration. I go from 'Miley Riley' to 'Miley Masen.' I am not sure that is an improvement."

"Maybe you could hyphenate. You could have the worst of both worlds," Travis proposed. "I know the perfect spot we could honeymoon."

"And where might that be?" Miley played along, already anticipating his answer.

"Why, right here in Oakley, of course," he motioned to the land in front of them. "I bet we could even get a family discount." He knew she would have her heart set on more exotic and expensive locales.

She turned within the cocoon of the sheet and his arms to face him. "We'll discuss it later," Miley answered, winking at him. She put her arms around Travis's shoulders and kissed him as the orange sun sank behind the purple clouds of night.

Jennifer Friess

 *The Riley Sisters*

New Adult Romance

Two different women.
Two different stories of small-town love...

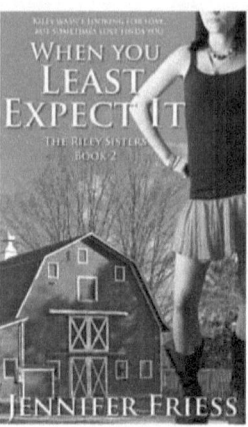

978-0692339565   978-0692452165

Available Now at Amazon, Barnes & Noble,
Kobo, iBooks, and others
ImNotStalkingYou.com

PATTI KENO

It all started with a kiss...

WHAT WOULD YOU DO IF A STRANGER STOLE YOUR BODY?

A SUPERNATURAL THRILLER AVAILABLE NOW IN PAPERBACK & EBOOK

JENNIFER FRIESS is an author, blogger, and editor who lives in Lenawee County, Michigan, with her husband, son, and dog. She loves entertainment trivia. She doesn't match her socks. She is a picky eater and likes it that way. Jennifer is the author of The Riley Sisters series, available now in paperback or on your favorite device.

Follow Jennifer here:

BLOG: ImNotStalkingYou.com
My mildly entertaining random thoughts

TWITTER: @jenf2

FACEBOOK: www.facebook.com/imnotstalkingyou2